SCARED STIFF

Other Apple Chillers
you will enjoy:

Christina's Ghost
by Betty Ren Wright

The Dollhouse Murders
by Betty Ren Wright

A Ghost in the House
by Betty Ren Wright

Ghost in the Noonday Sun
by Sid Fleischman

Ghosts Beneath Our Feet
by Betty Ren Wright

The Girl in the Window
by Wilma Yeo

The Magnificent Mummy Maker
by Elvira Woodruff

Scared to Death
by Jahnna N. Malcolm

SCARED STIFF

JAHNNA N. MALCOLM

SCHOLASTIC INC.
New York Toronto London Auckland Sydney

Special thanks to the Johnson family
and Dixon Rice for their help on this book.

ISBN 0-590-44996-6

20 19 18 17 16 15 14 5 6 7 8 9/9 0/0

Printed in the U.S.A. 40

To Bethany
This book is for you and because of you
with love and appreciation

SCARED STIFF

1

There is no way to get to my bedroom without passing a dead body. Go through the front door and you're staring right into a coffin in the chapel. Come in the back door and you're walking past the hearse, pickup van, and two viewing rooms. No one will ever come visit me and I don't blame them. If I didn't have to live here you couldn't pay me to walk through those front doors. But I do live here. With my brother Chace, and my parents — the morticians.

In the old days people like them were called undertakers. Chace, who thinks he is hysterically funny, calls them professional boxers. But however you label them, what they do is always the same — they prepare bodies for burial.

That gives me the creeps. I still don't understand why we have to live here at the funeral home. My father explains that it's traditional for morticians to live at the mortuary, plus it's easier for business. I tell him he ought to be in another line of business.

We live in this big old creaky mansion right in downtown Fairfield, Maryland. Most of the building — the main floor, garage, and basement — is used for the funeral home. We live upstairs on the second floor. It's terrible living in a mortuary. You always have to be quiet because someone might be downstairs viewing a body, or there might be a funeral going on.

When I was younger, I would stand by the door of a viewing room and stare at the body lying so still in its coffin. Sometimes I was sure I saw an eyelid flicker, or a chest rise and fall, as if the person had taken a breath. Then I'd run in a panic to get my mother.

"He's still alive!" I'd shout. "You can't let them bury him!"

Then my mother would take me by the hand and walk me down the carpeted stairs to the chapel and she would show me that it was impossible for Mr. Brown to be alive. She'd have me touch his hand and it would be cold.

"You see, Kelly," my mother would say, "this is just the shell of what used to be Mr. Brown. Our machines have removed his blood and replaced it with embalming fluid to preserve him."

Embalming fluid reeks. My father wears one of those blue surgical gowns when he works but sometimes a little bit of the fluid gets on his pants or shirt and it smells awful. That probably explains why he wears a lot of aftershave lotion. To cover the odor.

My brother, who at twelve is one year younger than me, loves living in a mortuary. He calls it the body shop and everyone laughs. Everyone except me. Lately it's gotten so bad that I can't bear to walk into the building. Even before I open the big wooden doors, I close my eyes. Then without looking I march past the chapel and the two viewing rooms to the foot of the staircase. I put my hand on the railing and start climbing. I don't open my eyes until I get to the top. That way, if there is a body downstairs, I won't have to look at it.

But I have to say — I *know* when there's a body there. I can feel its sightless eyes watching me.

Today there was no body on view but I hurried up to my room anyway. Things didn't feel right. Novembers are usually chilly and windy in Maryland but today there was no wind at all. The air seemed heavy and ominous, like something terrible was about to happen.

"Kelly?" my mother called through my locked door. "How was school?"

"Rotten," I grumbled. "I had a fight with Gretchen, I bombed a Spanish test, and two big zits showed up on my forehead."

"May I come in?"

I jumped off the bed, unlocked the door, then

threw myself back on my quilt. “Enter!”

Mom opened the door and came over and sat on my bed. She’s actually young and pretty but you’d never know it by the way she dresses — gray or brown suits, and pale pink or yellow blouses. And she pulls her thick hair into a bun at her neck. She’s says that’s what the customers expect in their mortician, someone solemn and serious.

“You’re going to be on your own for a while tonight,” Mom began. “Your father and I have to go to the Chamber of Commerce banquet.”

“Sounds dreary,” I muttered.

“I’m sure it will be,” she chuckled. “But the town’s honoring some of its older citizens, and your father thought we should attend. It’s — ”

“Good for business,” I finished with her in a singsong voice. “Don’t you ever do anything for fun?”

My mother cocked her head to look at me. “You’re not in a very cheery mood today.”

I shook my head.

“By the way, your brother is having a friend stay over,” my mother added, “so you’ll have some company.”

“Who?” I asked, pulling myself up on one elbow.

“Matt Avery.”

I wrinkled my nose. “Mom, he’s the biggest jerk in the seventh grade.”

My mother, who long ago mastered the art of always keeping a calm and pleasant look on her face, just shrugged. "I think he's a nice boy and he's funny. Why don't you like him?"

I really didn't know Matt very well. All I knew was that he was new at school and lived in an ugly old trailer behind Kroger's supermarket. But at that moment I was hating all boys over the age of two.

"If he's so great, why does he hang around with Chace, who is a whole year younger than him?"

"Because your brother is also very nice and extremely witty," my mother said.

"He thinks so," I murmured.

My mother patted my hand and stood up. That meant our discussion about Matt was over. "I charged a pizza from the Pizza Man and you can run down and rent a movie from Video Excitement if you like. We'll try to be back early but this could drag on and on."

I rolled over on my back and stared at the ceiling. "Have a good time."

My mother padded across the thick carpet to the door. "Why don't you call Gretchen or one of your other girlfriends, and have them stay over?" she suggested. "You could have fun."

"*What* girlfriends?" I shouted. "And who would want to stay overnight here? No girl I know would set foot in our house."

"Kelly." My mother sighed her ever-patient sigh. "I know it's difficult, and you must get teased a little — "

"A little!" I repeated sarcastically. "You don't know the half of it. The kids all act like I'm the one who does the embalming. And some of them won't even touch me."

"Oh, Kelly, that's just joking around."

"Some joke. They say our family must be a bunch of sickos to want to spend all day cutting up dead bodies."

"We don't do that, and you know it," my mom said sternly. "You also know that ours is a very necessary job. Every family in this town has needed our services at one time or another. They count on the Andersons to help them through a difficult time."

"Mom, don't give me that sales pitch," I groaned, putting the pillow over my head. "Save it for your customers."

Just then footsteps pounded up the stairs and my brother stuck his head in my room. "Mom, you should have seen Kelly today. She was incredible. She completely lost it in front of the entire lunchroom of Fairfield Middle School. I mean, we're talking major meltdown."

"I don't know what you're talking about," I said, narrowing my eyes at my brother and willing his lips to be sewn closed.

Chace munched away on a Snickers Bar as he

said, "One minute she's sitting with Gretchen, blabbing away, and the next minute, Kelly's shrieking at the top of her lungs."

"It wasn't that loud," I muttered, trying to block the entire episode out of my mind.

"Not that loud," Chace repeated. "I was all the way across the room and heard you clearly. The whole school did." He filled his mouth with the candy bar and said, "That would have been okay if you hadn't wimped out and started crying."

I could feel my face getting red all over again as I remembered the embarrassment of having the entire cafeteria go quiet and turn to stare at me. The rest of the school day had been a blur. All I wanted to do was go home and hide.

"*Oh*," my mother said as if she suddenly understood why I was so cranky. "I see."

I sat up on my bed and tried to keep my voice calm. "How can you see? Kids are always making cracks about me being an undertaker's daughter. I could take it when Gretchen was my friend. But now even she's turned against me."

"How has she turned against you?" my mother asked, sitting on the edge of my bed.

"She's started hanging around with that awful David Ensign."

"Who also happens to be Fairfield's ace striker on the soccer team," Chace explained to my mother, making it sound like I was jealous that Gretchen had a boyfriend when I didn't. Maybe he was a little bit right about that but I wasn't about to admit it.

"Well, David may be a big soccer star," I said to my brother. "But he's a mental midget. David told Gretchen my skin was cold and clammy from being around graves and dead people all the time."

Chace burst out laughing and nearly choked on his candy bar. It was gross. Peanuts and chocolate splattered everywhere. "That's a good one," he chortled. "I heard some kids say we're supposed to be vampires, too."

"What do you say to that?" my mother asked him.

Chace grinned, revealing the dimple in his cheek. "I tell them I *am*, and you'd better be careful, or I'll suck your blood and make you one, too." He wiggled his eyebrows as he talked in a thick accent like the Dracula in the movies. If I didn't want to hit him for telling Mom about the disaster at lunch, I probably would have laughed.

My mother did. Then she turned to me and said, "Why don't you try joking about it, Kelly? I bet people will laugh."

"That's just what Gretchen said."

"And that's why you fought?"

"We fought when she said I was a stubborn jerk."

"Hey, maybe Gretchen's not such a ditz after all," Chace said.

I threw my pillow at my brother and missed.

"Gretchen is supposed to be my best friend," I pointed out. "And be on my side when I need her the most."

"I wish we could talk more about this," my mother said, checking her watch. "Because I think we need to. But your father and I are due at the banquet in fifteen minutes."

"Where is Dad, anyway?" Chace asked, wiping his chocolate-covered hands on the T-shirt draped over the chair at my desk.

"I'm not sure," she replied. "But he knows he's supposed to be ready to leave here at six."

"Do you think he's gone on business?" Chace asked.

"I hope not," I said with a shudder. Whenever our family says *business*, it means that someone has died. And if that were true, that would mean I would have to spend the entire evening with my disgusting brother Chace, his weird friend Matt, and another dead body.

2

"Anderson Mortuary. You stab 'em, we slab 'em!" Chace bellowed into the telephone.

Luckily our home number is different from the office line. Still, he never would have answered that way if my parents had been home.

"Yeah, they're gone," Chace continued into the phone. "We've ordered pizza, pop, and a movie." He listened for a few more minutes and then said, "Just a minute, I'll ask. Kelly, do you know if Dad brought any stiffs in today?"

I hate it when he uses that word. It makes my skin crawl. "No," I said tightly, "I don't know. And you'd better not be going into the preparation room."

That's what we call the room where they get the bodies ready for burial. It is *always* kept locked. Unfortunately, about a year ago, Chace discovered where my father keeps the key. That's when he started giving tours of the prep room to his friends. If my parents ever found out about it, Chace would be grounded for *life*.

"Look, Matt, if there aren't any bodies, we can go look at the coffins," Chace suggested brightly. "See you." He hung up the phone and moved to the refrigerator. He took out a quart of milk and drank directly from the carton. "Matt'll be here in five minutes."

"I can hardly wait," I said, slipping onto one of the stools at the kitchen counter. "Why do you go into the prep room?"

"My friends like it," he said. "It's fun for them to get scared." He grabbed an apple from the bowl on the counter and sat down beside me. "Actually, I'm getting kind of bored with it. It's becoming the same old thing. I unlock the door and push them into the room. They take one look at the body lying there in the dark, I grab their neck — "

"You grab their neck?"

"Sure. That's what they're afraid of — that the body will come to life and get them. So I grab 'em, they scream, and run. The end."

He was so matter-of-fact about the whole thing that it made me laugh. Chace paused with his apple halfway to his mouth, a pleased smile on his face. "Hey, I made you laugh. It's a miracle."

"I laugh if the joke is funny," I replied, giving him a sour face. "It's just that lately I haven't felt like it much."

"No kidding." Chace filled his mouth with a

huge chunk of apple. "What's happened to you?"

"I'm not sure. But for the past month I've had this weird feeling inside, like when you haven't done your homework and you know that any minute the teacher is going to call on you and everything will be awful. I feel like something terrible is about to happen."

"What? Didn't you do your homework?" Chace asked.

I rolled my eyes. He'd missed my point completely. "It's not like that at all. It's something bigger, and more awful."

The doorbell rang, cutting off our conversation.

"I'll get it!" he bellowed as he raced for the stairs.

I followed my brother to the top of the landing and looked down into the foyer. The chandelier in the chapel was glowing a gentle amber. That was odd. Usually my parents turned out the lights when they were going away.

"Some go to heaven and some go to . . . hello!" Chace sang as he threw open the front door. I sighed loudly in disgust. Sometimes he thinks he is *sooo* funny.

Matt Avery stepped through the door, looking as scruffy as ever. He was wearing a beat-up leather jacket that was too big for him and a pair of jeans that were worn almost white at the knees.

A gust of cold air followed him inside and whooshed up the stairs, making me shiver. That, too, was strange, because not an hour before, the air outside had been still and warm, almost too warm for November.

"Wow, you should see what's happening out there," Matt said, shaking his head. Little droplets of water sprayed off his dark wavy hair. "The sky is filled with clouds that look like they're racing the Indy 500. Man, they are moving!"

I peered through the stained glass window on the landing and saw that Matt was right. Ugly dark clouds were streaming furiously across the sky and I suddenly got a weird tight feeling, like cold fingers were pressing against my spine.

"Chace," I called from the top of the stairs, "Mom and Dad left the light on in the chapel. Dad didn't bring a, um, customer in, did he?"

"Oh, cool, you mean you *did* get a stiff?" Matt rubbed his hands together expectantly.

"False alarm," Chace said as he ducked his head around the corner of the hall. "The red light's not on."

Matt looked crestfallen. "Too bad."

"Hey, I told you we'd check out the coffins after we eat," Chace reassured Matt as he flicked off the chandelier. "Don't you want to have some pizza first?"

"Yeah." Matt turned immediately and headed for the stairs. "I'm starved." He put his hand on the railing and smiled up at me. "Hi."

Matt had clear blue eyes and a tiny cleft in his

chin. If it weren't for the fact that he was so — so *different*, and hung around with younger guys like my brother, I would have thought he was pretty good-looking.

"The pizza's not here yet," I said coolly. "Mom only ordered it a little — "

There was a loud *thump* from the front door. It took me by such surprise that I yelped and put my hand over my mouth. "What was that?"

Matt shot me an amused look. "That's either a very big hailstone, or someone is announcing their arrival."

My brother opened the door and looked outside. Then he yelled, "Kelly, they did it again. Another airborne delivery."

"Airborne?" Matt asked, peering over Chace's shoulder.

"Yeah." Chace picked up a white box from the welcome mat. It was badly dented at one corner. "The guy Frisbeed our pizza at the front door."

"What guy?" Matt asked.

A screech of tires answered his question.

"There goes the Pizza Man," Chace said. "Scared out of his wits."

"The delivery guys are afraid to come here after dark," I explained from the stairs. "Just like everyone else in the town of Fairfield."

"You see, they think we're ghouls," Chace said in his Dracula voice. "We'll lure them into the embalming room and suck their blood."

Matt burst out laughing. "Chace, you are too weird for words." He picked up the crumpled pizza box and flipped back the lid. "Hey, the pizza looks okay." He scooped up a slice dripping with strings of melted cheese and took a bite. "Ummm! My favorite. Everything but the kitchen sink."

"Then let's chow down." Chace grabbed the box from Matt and the two of them ran up the stairs. They hurried past me into the den.

"Don't eat it all," I protested. "A third of that's mine, you know."

Fifteen minutes later, the pizza was gone. Chace and Matt practically inhaled the entire thing. I had to fight for the two pieces that I was able to grab for myself.

Shortly after Chace got Matt involved in a Nintendo duel, the grandfather clock in the downstairs foyer tolled the hour. I counted off the familiar chimes under my breath. Seven of them. Seven o'clock. I was about to turn back to my issue of *Seventeen* when I noticed the clock hadn't stopped ringing. *Bong. Bong. Bong.* It echoed eerily through the downstairs.

"Chace, that clock is goofing up again," I called from my armchair. "Go down and fix it."

The grandfather clock was Mom's special heirloom. It had been made by her great-grandfather, who was from Bavaria, and it looked like something out of a Grimms' fairy tale. Little trolls and gnomes were carved into the clock face. I thought they were very ugly.

"You do it," Chace muttered. "Can't you see I'm busy?"

I opened my mouth to complain but stopped. I didn't want Matt to know I was a chicken about going down into the chapel area alone. I could just imagine what the kids at school would say about me then. "Can you be-*lieve* it? Kelly Anderson's too scared to walk around her own house."

"Okay!" I shouted, slamming my magazine down in irritation. "I'll go."

Neither Chace nor Matt even noticed me leave the room. The foyer was inky black and there wasn't a trace of light. It was stupid to be scared of the dark. I knew it, but I still couldn't keep my pulse from racing. I took a deep breath and moved as fast as I could down the stairs with my arm extended in front of me. Then I bumped the light switch with my hand and the hall light went on.

Of course there was nothing there. I walked straight to the grandfather clock, which was still chiming away, and thumped the pendulum case hard with my fist. The gears groaned inside the old clock and it stopped ringing. Simple enough. I turned and marched back to the steps. I was halfway up the stairs when I sensed it.

There was a body in the building. I can always tell. But why did I feel it just now, instead of on the way downstairs? I backtracked until I could peer across the chapel into the hall beyond. A telltale red glow was coming from the light by the embalming room.

"Chace!" I shouted, running back to the second floor. "Chace!" I flew down the hall and burst into the family room and slammed the door behind me.

Chace glanced up from the video game and mumbled, "What?"

"I thought you said we didn't have any customers," I declared, putting my hands on my hips.

"We don't."

"Then why is the red light on in the prep room?"

"It isn't."

"Yes, it is. I was just downstairs and saw it."

"No way."

"Want to bet?" I demanded.

"Sure. A million dollars."

Matt leapt to his feet with a grin. "There's only one way to find out. Let's go see."

"You just want to stop the game because you're losing," Chace said, dropping his game controller onto the coffee table. "All right. Let's go check out the body shop."

I followed the boys into the hall but something made me hesitate at the top of the stairs. I just didn't feel like going down there.

"Maybe I was wrong," I muttered. "Let's go back. It was nothing."

"Come on!' Matt shouted, grabbing me by the

hand and pulling me down the stairs.

"Let go of me," I protested but Matt was surprisingly strong. He didn't let go of my hand until he had dragged me across the chapel and into the hallway on the far side of the building. The three of us stared at the red light shining like a beacon in the darkness above the locked embalming room.

"This is mondo-bizarro." Chace scratched his head. "I could have sworn that light was off."

"Does that mean someone's in there?" Matt said.

Chace nodded.

"What do they do with the bodies? Stuff 'em?"

"Of course not," I replied. "We have these machines that remove the blood and fill them with embalming fluid."

"All your blood? Like even in your eyes?"

"No, they yank out the eyes and put in marbles," Chace said wickedly.

"No eyes?" Even in the glow of the red light, Matt looked a little green.

"They do not," I protested. "Chace is just trying to scare you. The eyes stay but they put in these plastic eye caps under the lids."

"Then they wire the mouth shut so the jaw doesn't fall open," Chace continued.

Matt screwed up his face in disgust. "That is really gross."

Chace was really enjoying watching Matt squirm. He switched to his Dracula voice and, savoring each word, intoned, "After that they smear on this makeup that doesn't look like anything you've ever seen. It's purple."

"Why purple?"

"Blood is what gives skin its color," I explained, trying to keep my voice steady. "Once you take out the blood, the skin turns a whitish gray, like ashes."

"So this purple stuff makes the person look more alive," Chace concluded in his normal voice.

"I want to see it," Matt declared.

"What?"

"The body. I've never ever seen a dead one before."

Chace shrugged. "Okay."

"Chace, don't go in there," I warned.

"Why not?" Matt asked. "I'm just curious."

"For one thing, it's against the law for anyone other than a licensed mortician to be in there," I explained. "And besides, it's just not right. The body could've been in an accident and be all messed up. Do you really want to see something *that* awful?"

Matt nodded enthusiastically. "You bet."

Chace hesitated. "Maybe Kelly's right. It's not like Dad to drop one of them off without telling us."

"No one will ever have to know," Matt said. He put his hand on his heart. "I won't tell and I'm sure Kelly won't. So why are you worrying?"

Chace shook his head. "I don't know. Maybe it's this strange-O weather, or something. I just feel, I don't know — funny."

Matt folded his arms and stared at him.

"All right," Chace said with a sigh. "I'll get the key. But we can't stay in the room for more than a minute. We'll cruise in and cruise out."

"I can't believe you're doing this," I muttered as my brother returned with the key and inserted it into the lock. "What if Mom and Dad come home?"

"They won't be home for hours." He turned the key and the lock clicked.

"Well, if you think I'm going to stick around out here and wait for you two to get grossed out," I said, "you can forget it. I'm going back upstairs to my room and lock the door."

Neither one of them answered me. Matt's face was flushed with excitement as the door swung open.

"After you," Chace said, gesturing into the dim interior of the room.

"This is too cool!" Matt said in a hushed voice. He stepped inside and Chace followed. The door slid shut behind them and I was alone in the hall.

3

I hurried to my bedroom and slammed the door. I was angry and scared. Angry at Chace for going into the embalming room. Angry at my father for not telling me he'd brought in a body. But mostly I was scared. The cold air that had swept in the front door with Matt Avery seemed to have given me a permanent case of goose bumps.

Chace later told me that while I fumed upstairs, he and Matt stood silently inside the embalming room, which was lit by a single dim bulb above the porcelain sink in the corner. The shapes of the different objects in the room threw looming shadows against the wall.

"This looks like the operating room at a hospital," Matt murmured.

"Yeah, sometimes my parents call it that," Chace replied. "See, it has two work stations." He pointed to a long stainless steel gurney, with a smaller cart resting alongside it. A metal canister sat on the cart with a pair of long tubes coiled around it. Shelves filled with jars and bottles of chemicals lined the wall of the room.

One stainless steel table stood empty and gleaming. But the one against the wall had something lying on it, covered with a white sheet.

"Is that a dead body?" Matt whispered, as if he were afraid his own voice might disturb it.

"Yep. It sure is."

Chace flicked the switch by the door and the fluorescent lights hummed to life. The bright glare made both of them blink for a few seconds. Matt saw the pair of bare feet sticking out from under the sheet and shuddered. The toes were crabbed and mottled, with long yellow nails.

"Whoa, check out those feet," Matt murmured. "They're gross."

"He's definitely an old geezer," Chace observed without moving from the doorway.

Matt pointed to the big toe on the left foot. "There's something tied around his toe."

"That's his identification tag," Chace explained. "When people die in hospitals or public institutions, the coroner always tags 'em before they're sent to us. That way they don't get mixed up."

Matt inched toward the feet and cocked his head to read the tag. "It says his name is J. L. Torbett."

As he watched his friend examine the tag, Chace toyed with the idea of playing his usual prank of shutting off the lights and grabbing him by the neck. He decided against it. Something didn't feel right.

"Let's look under the sheet," Matt said, not taking his eyes off the body.

"Go ahead."

Matt shot Chace a nervous look. "You lift the sheet up."

"Why can't you?" Chace asked. "You're closer."

"Yeah, but you're used to this stuff."

"What, are you scared?" Chace teased.

He fully expected Matt to bristle and deny it. Instead his friend surprised him by saying, "Of course I'm scared." Matt put his hands on his hips. "What do you think I am, some kind of idiot? I mean, old J. L. here could be a zombie, or have died of the plague, or be missing his head, or something majorly disgusting like that."

"No way." Chace inched up beside his friend. "His head's still there. I can see the shape of his nose."

"Pull back the sheet," Matt whispered. "We'll just take a quick look and then leave. I'm starting to get the creeps."

"Well, if you'd just stop thinking about the plague and zombies," Chace said, grabbing the corner of the sheet with his hand, "and just think of this corpse as some old guy who probably died in his sleep, you'd feel a lot better." Chace pulled the sheet back with a casual flick of his wrist, as if he did it a hundred times a day.

Matt leapt backwards with his eyes closed, but nothing happened. Finally he squeezed open one eye and stared down at the face of the body tagged as J. L. Torbett.

A white-haired old man with craggy features lay with his hands folded across his chest. The boys stared in fascination at the impassive features. His closed eyes lay half hidden in the deep shadows of his eye sockets. Two dark eyebrows flecked with silver arched up across his forehead. A ragged stubble of beard dotted his cheeks and chin. His lips were slightly parted as if he had been on the verge of saying something when he died.

"Why's he wearing that orange jumpsuit?" Matt asked. "Don't they usually wear black suits and ties?"

Chace peered down at the old man. "They must have just brought him in. But it's odd . . ." His voice trailed off.

"What?" Matt shot his friend a worried look. "What's wrong?"

"Well, usually when Dad brings in a body he cancels his other plans and gets right to work on it. This man hasn't been touched."

"You mean, they haven't drained his blood yet?"

Chace shook his head.

Matt stared intently at the dead man's face. "How do they do it?"

"Dad mixes the stuff up from those chemicals on the shelves." Chace uncoiled one of the long tubes and held it up. "Then he sticks a long needle, sort of like what you use to blow up a basketball, into the guy's veins and — "

"*Oooooooohh.*"

A sound like a mooing cow suddenly sounded behind the boys.

Chace, who was busy recoiling the tube around its canister, turned his head to Matt and asked, "Did you make that sound?"

Matt didn't answer. His eyes were two huge circles in his face. His jaw flopped up and down but no sound came out.

Chace turned to look at the corpse. His heart was beating a little faster but he kept his voice calm. "Don't panic, Matt. What we just heard was air escaping from the body. It happens all the time."

Matt's voice was a hoarse croak. "Oh." He chuckled nervously and added, "I thought the guy was talking."

"No way." Chace strolled nonchalantly over to the gurney. "Believe me, J. L. Torbett has spoken his last words." He grabbed the edge of the sheet and tossed it back over the body's face.

Another low groan came from the corpse. Both boys stepped back and then watched in horror as the figure draped in white slowly sat up.

"He — he's *alive*!" Matt clutched Chace's arm

and yanked him backwards. Chace lost his balance and fell against the empty gurney, sending it crashing against the far wall.

Matt backed for the door shouting, "Kelly! Help! Come quick!"

Chace plastered himself against the sink and stared at the body sitting on the gurney. The corpse's sudden movement had startled him but he wasn't really frightened. He remembered that sometimes after a person dies, the nerves shoot off electro-chemical impulses that make the muscles twitch and jerk like a body is still alive, when it's really not.

Once we had to kill a copperhead snake that got into the backyard. Dad cut off its head with a shovel so we knew the horrible thing was dead. But for almost an hour afterwards, whenever Chace flipped the headless body over with a stick, the snake would writhe and coil.

Remembering this kept Chace from panicking. It was what happened next that made my brother's hair stand on end.

The corpse's head slowly turned to face my brother and the deep set eyes popped open. Two yellow eyes glared at him. The mouth moved soundlessly and then one bony hand reached out from under the sheet and pawed the air.

That did it. Chace's eyes rolled back in his head and his knees buckled beneath him. He hit the floor with a loud thud.

4

"Chace! Are you okay?" I shouted as I ran down the hall toward the prep room. Matt's cries for help had brought me out of my room and down the stairs.

"Wha — what happened?" I heard Chace mumble from the floor. He sounded a little groggy.

I reached the door and saw a huge white-haired man in an orange jumpsuit swaying in the center of the room. One hand was on his forehead, and the other groped for the wall as he tried to get his balance.

"Who are you?" I demanded. "What do you think you're doing here?"

Matt grabbed my arm and pulled me out of the room. "The guy's a corpse," he whispered hoarsely. "He's dead."

"Get off it," I hissed back. "He's walking and mumbling. That's not dead."

"Five minutes ago, he was lying on that table stiff as a board," Matt sputtered. "I'm telling you,

Kelly, he's a zombie or a ghost or something."

I hurried back into the room and knelt down beside Chace, being careful to steer clear of the old man, who was making little growling sounds in his throat as he steadied himself.

"You're okay, Chace." I slipped my hands under my brother's shoulders and propped him up. "You just fainted, that's all."

Matt came into the room and grabbed Chace's arms and pulled him to a standing position. "Get up," he muttered under his breath. "And let's get out of here. Now!"

Chace stumbled to his feet and Matt and I dragged him toward the door.

"No . . . one . . . going . . . anywhere." The words blasted out of the man's throat in fits and starts. We all froze in our tracks.

The man with the white hair and red eyes may have been old but he was still really big, at least six feet tall. He stood with his arms spread wide across the doorsill, totally blocking our escape. "Stay . . . *back*."

Chace was fully conscious by now. "You can't scare me," he declared. "You're dead. You have no power."

"Dead?" This information seemed to come as a big surprise to the man. He blinked his eyes thoughtfully. Then in that gravelly voice he tried the word again. "Dead."

Before Chace could explain about their discovering him lying on the gurney with the tag on his toe, Matt jumped in and said, "If you're not dead, how did you get in here?"

"I'm . . . not sure." The man scratched his head and then struggled for the words. "I was in my . . . cell. Closed . . . my eyes. Now . . . here."

"Cell!" I repeated. "You mean, like in prison?" I turned to Matt and Chace and hissed, "This is worse than a zombie. That guy is an escaped criminal."

The old man's head jerked up and he snapped, "I am *not* a criminal."

"That's what they all say," Matt mumbled under his breath.

"No whispering!" The man bellowed with such force that all three of us took a step backwards. After that shout, he was going to have to do a lot of talking to convince me that he wasn't a guilty convict.

The three of us huddled together and watched the man slowly become aware of his surroundings. He rubbed his eyes and then blinked up at the harsh work lights on the ceiling. "Where am I?"

"You're at Anderson Mortuary," Chace answered. Then he added in a timid voice, "Mr. Torbett."

The man shot him a suspicious look. "How do you know my name?"

"It's on the tag." Chace pointed at the man's bare feet. "J. L. Torbett."

The man lifted his foot and stared at the tag. "What is this, a joke?"

"You don't see me laughing," I murmured.

Torbett put his foot back on the tile floor and slowly raised his head. His lips barely moved as he asked, "What town is this?"

"It's Fairfield, Maryland," Chace answered.

"Fairfield!" He closed his eyes for a second and took a deep breath. "And the day?"

"November thirteenth." I remembered because today was a Friday and everyone at school had been talking about what bad luck it was to have a Friday the thirteenth. Of course having an escaped convict hold you hostage in your own house wasn't just bad luck, it was a *curse*.

The man named Torbett heard the date and it was like a jolt of electricity shot threw him. His head flew back and his nostrils flared with excitement. I almost expected to see sparks come shooting out of his eyes. "My time has come."

"What do you mean?" I asked. Now I was convinced that we were not only being held prisoner by an escaped criminal, but a lunatic, too.

"Fifty years in a cell. Planning my revenge. Fifty years." He turned his massive head toward us and his yellow eyes flashed. "Fifty years to the day."

"You spent fifty years in prison?" I asked. He must have done something really terrible to get a sentence like that.

"For a murder I didn't commit." Just the idea of it seemed to anger him and he swung his arm at one of the shelves, knocking an entire row of glass bottles to the floor. One of the bottles broke on the shelf and a large shard of glass lodged in the back of his hand.

Matt dug his elbow into my side and hissed, "Look at his hand. It's not bleeding."

It was true. To top it off, the man didn't seem to notice that he had been cut. He stared down at the bottles strewn around his feet and moaned, "Revenge. I want revenge."

I summoned my courage and asked, "Revenge on whom?"

"All of them." He raised his head and stared into the air as if he were seeing the people in front of him. "Judge Michael Keedy sentenced me. Clara Simpson convicted me. And Harlan Cody double-crossed me. He was the key witness."

Chace cocked his head. "Wait a minute. How could one person convict you? Aren't there twelve jurors?"

"Eleven are dead." His lips curled back in a grotesque smile. "Soon Clara will join them."

This time I turned to Matt and without moving my lips hissed, "Did you hear that? He's planning on killing someone."

A sharp pain shot through my foot as Chace stomped on it. I almost cried out but bit my lip to keep quiet when I realized why Chace had done that.

J. L. Torbett was staring at me with those terrible red eyes. His breath made a wheezy sound as it moved across his vocal cords. "No one. . . . *No one* . . . will stop me!"

"I wouldn't think of it," I whispered.

J. L. Torbett moved toward me in a stiff-legged stride as if he weren't quite used to walking. His lips were twisted in a permanent snarl and his voice was only a hideous wheeze. "No one gets in my way."

I backed up, trying to put the steel gurney between me and him. He just kept coming and for a second I saw my life pass before my eyes.

"Hey, Torbett!" Matt called suddenly from across the room. "The door's over here."

The old man spun and lost his balance for a fraction of a second. That's when Chace yelled, "Kelly, run for it!"

I pushed the gurney against the man's body and tried to make a dash for the door. But a hand with glass sticking out of it grabbed my arm. The skin was cold and gray. I looked into Torbett's eyes and saw absolutely no flicker of life in them.

All at once I knew that Matt could be right. Maybe Torbett wasn't alive. Maybe he really had come back from the dead.

"Let go of her!" Chace bellowed. In a mighty leap, he jumped on the back of the old man and started pounding him with his fists.

"No one stops me," the man growled, swinging his arms out to shake Chace off his back. "No one!"

Chace flew across the room like a rag doll. He hit the wall with a loud "Oomph!" and slumped to the floor.

Then Torbett turned on Matt, who stood framed in the doorway. He was poised with his knees bent, his arms cocked in front of him, as if he were ready for a fight. Torbett ran for him but, at the last moment, Matt dropped to the floor. The huge man tripped over Matt's body and went flying through the door into the corridor.

"Shut it!" I yelled. "Shut the door!"

Chace scrambled over on his hands and knees and the two of us collided trying to get the door closed. Matt's ankle was stuck between the door and the jamb and he howled, "Wait, my foot!"

I jerked his foot free just as Chace slammed the door shut.

"Lock it, Chace!" I shouted.

"I can't," he replied. "It locks from the other side. The key's still in the dead bolt."

"Brace yourself!" Matt ordered.

The three of us hunched our shoulders against the door and waited for Torbett to ram it. But nothing happened.

"Do you think he's gone?" I whispered after several minutes.

Matt shook his head. "I didn't hear him walk

away. I think he's still out there, waiting for us to drop our guard."

"There are three of us and he's just an old man," Chace said in a shaky voice. "He couldn't knock down the door, could he? It's impossible, right?"

"Like a corpse coming back to life is possible?" Matt muttered.

"This has got to be a dream," Chace whispered. "It's a dream and any second I'm going to wake up."

I held my breath and hoped that somehow he was right, that maybe we would wake up back in the family room, with the boys playing video games and me reading my magazine.

"That guy couldn't really be a corpse, could he?" Chace babbled. "A walking zombie? Those things don't really happen, do they?"

"I don't know what to think," Matt answered. "All I know is what I saw. A body under a sheet who was deader than a doornail sat up and spoke to us. He looked like an old man but had the strength of three young men. He said he went to prison for a murder he didn't commit and now he wants — "

"Revenge!" The horrible wheeze seemed to seep through the keyhole and fill the room. Then we heard the sound of the bolt sliding shut, followed by a grotesque chuckle.

We listened to his footsteps drag along the carpet in the hall. The front door creaked open and

I heard the whine of the wind as it rushed into the foyer. Then the door shut and there was silence.

"He's gone," Matt announced with a sigh of relief. He slid to the floor and put his head in his hands. "That thing is gone."

"Yes," Chace said, twisting the door knob. "But he's locked the only door out of this room."

Matt jerked his head up sharply. "You mean . . . ?"

I nodded. "We're trapped."

5

"Oh, no!" I suddenly gasped. "Gretchen!"

"What about her?" Chace asked as he tried to pick the lock with a paper clip.

"She's baby-sitting for Mr. and Mrs. Keedy tonight. The old judge lives with his grandson now. Torbett is going to go there." I threw open the cupboard that my father used for a desk. There was a phone tucked in the top drawer. I grabbed the receiver. "I've got to call her."

Before I could even push one of the buttons, Matt had grabbed it out of my hands.

"What do you think *you're* doing?" I demanded.

"Calling the cops, of course," he replied as he punched in 911. "They're a lot better equipped to deal with this than we are."

"But we've got to warn Gretchen — "

"The cops will be at that house in minutes," he said. Someone must have answered at the other end because Matt lowered his voice and tried to sound mature. "Yes, I'd like to report a murderer on the loose. And he's — what? Oh. Sure. My name is Matthew Avery. My address . . . well, at the moment I'm locked in the embalming room at the Anderson Mortuary — no, this is *not* a joke."

"Let me have that." I yanked the phone out of his hand. "Hello, this is Kelly Anderson of Anderson's Mortuary. It's true, we *are* in the embalming room. A deceased body locked us in here. But don't worry about us. Please, you've got to send the police over to the Keedy residence where my friend Gretchen is baby-sitting."

Matt rolled his eyes at the ceiling. "Oh, that's much more convincing," he whispered sarcastically. "I bet they're putting the SWAT team right on it."

I put my finger in my ear and closed my eyes to shut him out. Meanwhile the operator's voice whined in my ear, saying, "I just want you to know, young lady, that it is a crime to make prank calls on this emergency line. You should be ashamed of yourself."

"I'm deadly serious," I exploded.

"Give me your name again," the lady demanded. "I think your parents should know what you're up to."

"You are an idiot!" I shouted into the phone. "And because of your stupid pigheadedness several innocent people might lose their lives tonight." I slammed down the phone and screamed with frustration.

"That's telling her," Matt said, folding his arms nonchalantly. "I guess now we'll be saved."

I narrowed my eyes at him angrily. "You started the whole thing off on the wrong foot by saying we were locked in the embalming room, you jerk."

Matt turned to my brother and asked, "Is your sister always this charming?"

I ignored his crack and, grabbing the phone book, tried to look up the Keedys' phone number. My hands were shaking so badly I could barely flip through the thin pages. When I finally found the right page and dialed the number, I was answered by a steady beep-beep on the line.

"Busy!" I shouted in frustration. "Gretchen is the biggest blabbermouth I have ever known. Once she gets the phone in her ear, you practically have to operate to remove it."

I dialed the number again. This time the busy signal seemed even louder and more irritating. I threw the phone down on the desk and bellowed, "Chace! When are you going to get that stupid door unlocked?"

"Maybe never." Chace straightened up and looked at the bent piece of metal in his hands. "I don't get it. These things work like a charm for the movie detectives."

"Why don't you just take the door off its hinges?" I demanded.

“That would work fine except it hinges from the outside,” Matt said, pulling the one metal chair out from the wall and standing on it.

“Then let’s break it down!” I shouted.

Chace looked up from the doorknob. “With what? My bulging biceps?”

I put my hands on my hips. “What’s the matter with you two? Don’t you realize there’s some kind of psycho out there?”

“Yes, Kelly, we do,” Matt replied, “but there’s no use getting hysterical about it.” He pushed up one of the acoustical tiles in the ceiling and stood on tiptoe trying to peer into the space inside. We can’t get out through the ceiling.”

“I could have told you that,” I said, crossing my arms. “Dad put in that false ceiling for ventilation. There’s just a fan up there and that’s it.”

Matt hopped off the chair and slapped the dust off his hands. “Well, one thing we can be happy about — ”

“What?” I cut in.

“As long as Torbett is out there, I can’t think of a safer place for us to be than locked in here.”

“I was thinking the same thing,” Chace agreed.

“But he has the key,” I reminded them. “He could burst in here at any time and we’d be trapped like rats in a cage.”

“Your sister’s got a point.” Matt scratched his chin. His eyes widened and he moved to the wall directly in front of him and knocked hard three times.

"It's no good knocking," Chace said. "No one will hear you. The outside walls are made out of brick."

He continued knocking and the sounds went abruptly from a solid thud to a hollow sound. "Then what's that?" Matt asked.

"That's where Dad sealed up the window." Chace joined Matt and traced a thin seam that bordered a wide rectangle in the wall. "It was right here. He didn't want people peering in to see who he was working on. So he boarded it up."

Matt banged his fist against the wall again. "These are just plain boards?"

Chace nodded. "Plywood, actually."

"Then what are we waiting for?" Matt said, clapping his hands together. He gestured to me. "Get something to cut through here."

"Like what?" Chace asked. "A chain saw? I just happen to have one in my pocket."

"If you just want something to cut with," I said to Matt, "Dad keeps the scalpels in that metal cabinet." I pointed to the two-drawer cabinet on wheels resting in the corner.

"Thanks." Matt smiled at me. "Let's try them."

Chace found two scalpels in a tray in the top drawer. The boys each took one of the sharp thin blades and started digging at the edges of wall.

"All right!" Matt crowed as big chips of wood fell to the tiled floor. "It's working."

I tried the Keedys' number once more. "Still busy." I bit my lip anxiously and muttered, "Gretchen! Shut up and get off the phone."

"She's probably talking to David," Chace said.

"Try calling the other people Torbett mentioned," Matt suggested. "Like Harlan Cody and Clara, uh . . . somebody."

"Simpson," Chace mumbled without looking up from the hole he was chiseling into the wall.

"Who?"

"The woman's name is Clara Simpson."

I flipped first to the C's and thumbed down the list of names. "Harlan Cody isn't listed."

"That figures," Matt said. "The old guy probably doesn't even have a phone."

"Do you know him?" I asked.

"I know who he is, and where he lives." Matt made a sour face. "It's an absolute dump."

"Try Clara Simpson," Chace said. I quickly looked up the number for Miss Simpson. This time I got a ringing tone. "Well, at least her phone's not busy," I said. "I hope she's home."

"Sure she'll be home," Matt said. "Someone her age probably never leaves the house." His voice seemed calm but his movements were quick as he jabbed at the wall with the scalpel.

"Do you know her, too?"

"No, but figure it out. She was a juror on a trial fifty years ago. She's got to be in her 70's or 80's by now."

"Or dead," Chace said.

Just mentioning "dead" sent another one of those cold, spidery feelings up my spine. I listened to the phone ring eight times and finally a feeble voice answered, "Hello?"

"Miss Simpson? This is Kelly Anderson."

"I don't know any Kelly Anderson."

"I know that. But you might know my parents — Arthur and Marie Anderson?"

"No, I don't." The old lady's voice started to sound irritated. "Look, are you trying to sell me Girl Scout cookies or magazines, because I'm not interested."

"No, Miss Simpson, please — "

"The Kiwanis know how I feel about their spaghetti dinners and if you're trying to pawn off a set of those expensive light bulbs for the handicapped, save your breath. I can barely walk myself."

"Miss Simpson!" I shouted into the phone to try to get her to stop talking. It seemed to work and when she paused, I quickly said, "Don't take this wrong, but I have reason to suspect that your life may be in danger."

"What in the world are you talking about?"

I took a deep breath and said, "J. L. Torbett."

"Now see here, young lady, if that's a joke, I'm not laughing."

"It's no joke, Miss Simpson." I tried to keep my voice steady. "Torbett has, um, escaped and now he wants revenge — "

"I'm calling the police and having you arrested," the woman cut in. "This is sick, absolutely sick!"

"Please, Miss Simpson!"

I thought I heard something like the sound of glass breaking in the background behind the old lady's voice. But I couldn't be sure because at the same moment Matt and Chace managed to wrench one of the boards loose from the window with a loud crack. I covered my other ear to hear what Miss Simpson was saying.

"Who are you?" she shrieked. "If you've come to repair my water heater, it's not broken."

"I told you I'm Kelly Anderson and I'm trying to warn you," I replied. "Don't you see?"

"And no, I don't want any vacuum cleaner demonstrations!"

"I won't bother you anymore if — "

"How did you get in here?"

I suddenly realized Miss Simpson wasn't talking to me. Someone had broken into her house and was after her.

"He's there!" I hissed to the boys. "He's already found Clara Simpson."

They froze in their tracks, their eyes huge with

fear. The tinny sound of the old woman's voice pierced the awful silence of the room. We stood helplessly as she cried, "Stay away from me!"

I couldn't stand it any longer. "Run, Clara," I screamed into the phone. "Get out of the house and run!"

But it was too late. The line was dead.

6

"We've got to help that poor woman!" I shouted at Matt and Chace.

"I don't think anyone can help her now," Matt said as he pulled the last piece of plywood away from the window. "All we can do is try and warn the others."

Clara Simpson's cries for help were still ringing in my head as I tried to dial Gretchen once more. The horrible beep-beep droned from the receiver. "This is making me crazy. Why won't she get off the phone?"

"Because she's an airhead," Chace replied. Normally I would have defended Gretchen, but at that moment I agreed with my brother.

The window was now clear and Matt grabbed the stainless steel gurney that only a little while ago had held the body of J. L. Torbett, and rolled it as far from the window as he could. "Stand back!" he called.

Chace and I turned our backs as Matt pushed

the gurney toward the exposed window with all his might. The crash sent bits of glass showering onto the floor but jagged shards remained stuck in the windowpane.

"We can't climb through that," I said. "It'll cut us to ribbons."

Matt grabbed the sheet that had covered Torbett and wrapped it hurriedly around his forearm. He punched at the shards until they were completely broken off. "That's it."

A gust of cold air came into the room through the broken window. "Brrr!" I said, shivering from the sudden chill.

"Put one of these on." Matt tossed me one of the blue surgical gowns hanging on a hook on the back of the locked door. "It's not a coat but it's layering. It should keep you warm."

I held the blue hospital gown at arm's length and crinkled my nose. Matt saw my reaction, then shot Chace a baffled look.

"What's her problem?"

"That's one of my dad's work aprons," Chace explained.

"So?"

"So it's probably got blood and *viscera* on it," Chace said. He saw Matt's baffled look and explained, "That's the scientific name for guts."

Suddenly I felt really silly for being so squeamish. "Give it to me," I snapped. "I'll wear it." I slipped my arms into the sleeves and tried to keep my skin from crawling.

"Now what?" Chace asked after he and I had put on the blue gowns.

"Grab anything you can find to use as a weapon," Matt ordered.

"What do we need weapons for?" I asked. "You're not seriously planning to fight Torbett, are you?"

"Of course not," Matt said, kneeling down by the sink and opening the cabinet doors. "But if we run into him I don't intend to be totally helpless."

He pulled out all of the plastic embalming tubes and slung them over his shoulder. I opened the drawers of the metal cabinet and grabbed several scalpels and a roll of thin cord and handed them to Matt. I found a flashlight under the sink and tucked it into my gown's pocket.

Matt scrambled up onto the ledge of the window and held out his hand to me. "Come on, let's go."

Moments later the three of us stood on the lawn outside the mortuary. A thick mist choked the streetlights, making it really hard to see. The familiar street in front of our house looked strange and eerie in the shifting shadows.

"What's the plan?" Chace asked, with a shiver.

"I say we go to that awards banquet and get your parents," Matt said.

"No way!" I cried. "Are you forgetting about

Gretchen? She's baby-sitting at the Keedys'. What if Torbett goes there next? We've got to warn her."

"I think Kelly's right," Chace said.

Matt hesitated for only a moment. Then he nodded and said, "Okay, but we just tell her what's happening, and then we get out of there."

He was about to head down the street when I grabbed him by the arm. "Let's take our bikes," I said. "It'll be faster."

Matt slapped his forehead with his hand. "Why didn't I think of that? Mine's by the front door. Where are yours?"

"In the garage," Chace replied.

"I'll meet you in the driveway. Hurry!"

Chace and I raced for the garage behind our house. The mist was swirling around the windows and I could barely see the outline of the building. The little side door was half open and the ink-black interior loomed ominously. The possibility of Torbett the corpse lurking in the shadows inside nearly stopped my heart with fear.

"Chace?" I whispered to my brother. "Would you get mine? I'm too scared to go in there."

Normally Chace would have teased me about being a scaredy-cat. This time he slipped his hand in mine and said in a shaky voice, "Why don't we go in together?"

I felt a little safer holding my brother's hand. But not much. We ran as fast as we could inside the garage, grabbed the handlebars of our bikes, and jerked them out onto the driveway. I bumped my head hard against a sled hanging from the rafters but barely felt it. I was too numb with fear.

Then we pedaled out onto the road and stopped under the first streetlight. Matt came rolling out of the fog and pulled to a stop beside us. "Do you know the way to the Keedys' house?" He spoke in a whisper as if that corpse were nearby and might hear us.

"It's on Mulberry Hill," I replied. "The big white house at the top."

"That's on the other side of town." Matt scratched his chin. With the embalming tubes looped over his shoulder and the other stuff he'd gathered up tied in a surgical gown on his back, he looked like some sort of weird mountain climber. "We'll take a shortcut through the Addition."

I made a sour face. The Addition was the worst part of town. It was originally built to house migrant workers when they came for the fall harvest. Now it was mostly tumbledown shacks and boarded-up buildings. No one went there after dark if they could possibly avoid it.

"Do we have to?" I said. "That place gives me the creeps."

"Me, too," Matt replied. "And I live there."

I'd forgotten about that. My cheeks grew hot

with embarrassment and I stammered, "Sorry, I-I just meant—"

Matt didn't let me finish. "I know it's not that safe. So stay close and pedal faster than you ever have before. Torbett's on foot. We should be able to outrun him."

"*It*," Chace corrected him. "Remember, he's just a body."

"A body who could be out killing people," Matt added.

"Bodies only come to life on Saturday morning cartoons," I murmured, half to myself. "I don't understand what's happening."

"There are a lot of things that happen in this world that you just can't explain," Matt said as he led us onto Taylor Street, a pretty avenue lined with huge old elms that made a canopy of branches.

I tried to suppress a shiver. This was the last nice street before we entered the Addition.

"Maybe Torbett isn't really a corpse," Chace suggested. "Maybe he's just an escaped criminal who faked his death to get out of prison."

"Whatever he is," Matt said, "he's dangerous."

We rounded the corner and the pavement turned to gravel. It was as if someone had suddenly turned out all the lights. Most of the streetlights were broken or burnt out. The first house we passed had a broken window covered up with a pair of wooden planks. In the driveway was a rusty old car resting on concrete cinder blocks. A scrawny dog gnawed on something by the front bumper. He raised his head to watch us go by and his eyes glowed like red coals in the reflection from the tiny house's porch light.

"Like I said," Matt murmured, "stay close."

"Gretchen, lock the doors," I said with each push on my bike's pedals. "Lock the doors. Lock the doors. Lock the doors." The words became a chant. It made me feel a little bit better to concentrate on my friend and not on my own heart, which was thundering in my ears.

"Look out!" Matt shouted as a cat leapt into the road. Chace braked hard to miss running over it. He skidded sideways and his front wheel bounced against the curb. For a moment I was sure he was going to be thrown to the ground but he regained control and came safely to a stop.

"I nearly bought it on that one," Chace muttered as Matt and I pulled up alongside of him. In spite of the cold, a thin line of sweat beaded his forehead, and I knew he was really shaken up.

"Maybe we should go a little slower," I said. "Otherwise one of us could really get hurt."

"Okay." Matt knelt down by Chace's front wheel and ran his hand along the rim. "It's not bent." As he straightened up, Matt added, "Harlan Cody lives on this street. Should we try to warn him first?"

"He lives on this street?" My throat constricted

and I choked out, "That means T-T-Torbett could be here."

"Torbett?" Chace hopped back onto his bike. "Let's get out of here."

My common sense screamed at me to get out of there as fast as possible. But my conscience knew that we had to warn Harlan Cody. "Where's the house?" I asked Matt.

"Over there." He pointed to a tiny house stuck between two abandoned buildings. The barren yard was littered with rusted auto parts, crumpled garbage cans, and yellowed newspapers. A dim light shone through a side window. "I'll talk to him. You two keep guard."

"I don't like this, I don't like this at all," Chace said as we rolled our bikes through the junk to the front porch. The front step was missing and one of the posts along the sagging porch had two empty coffee cans holding it up.

"Keep an eye out for anything funny out there," Matt hissed as he stepped up to the front door and rapped sharply.

While we waited I stared into the darkness. The mist curled around every shadow, playing funny tricks on my eyes. Every time I blinked it seemed as if something out there moved.

"Did you see that?" Chace gasped, grabbing my arm.

I strained to see what he was looking at. "What?"

He pointed to the trunk of a dead tree on the opposite side of the street. The broken windows of the abandoned houses glittered eerily behind it. I held my breath and listened for any sound. All was still.

"There's nothing there," I whispered.

Then something moved in the shadows to the right of the tree trunk. I dug my nails into Chace's arm and turned to warn Matt. But before I could say a thing, the door of the shack swung open.

The cold steel barrel of a shotgun was thrust into Matt's face.

"Get inside," a voice twanged, "before I set your eyes spinning in your little pinheads."

7

None of us felt like arguing with a shotgun. We filed silently into the front room of the tiny house. Harlan Cody, a thin crusty old man in a greasy undershirt and stained green work pants, squinted at us. Most of his teeth were missing and his eyes had that blue cloudy look old people get when they have cataracts. Harlan shut the door behind us and turned the lock.

"Mr. Cody—" Matt started to say but the old man turned on him.

"Nobody does any talkin'," Harlan said in his thick southern accent, "until I say so."

We huddled together in the living room, which was hardly big enough to hold the four of us. A green couch with only one back cushion was pushed up against the widest wall. Some yellowed sheets and a brown wool blanket lay in a crumpled heap upon it. The couch obviously served as the man's bed. An ancient metal TV tray held a beat-up television set with a bent coat hanger for an antenna. Ashtrays made out of tuna fish cans overflowing with cigarette butts lay on stacks of magazines all over the room. The whole place smelled awful.

Harlan flicked on the overhead light and then smiled a toothless grin. "Now I'd like you to tell me just what you think you were doing on my porch."

"We've come to warn you, Mr. Cody," Matt said. "J. L. Torbett is looking for you."

The old man's eyes widened for a second. Then he pulled his withered frame up to its full height and squinted at us suspiciously. "Who told you about him?"

Matt decided to skip the part of the story where Torbett was lying dead in the mortuary. "We, uh, accidentally ran into him tonight," he said carefully, "and he was raving about getting revenge on everyone who put him in prison. He mentioned your name."

Harlan didn't question Matt. Instead he moved to the front window, lifted the torn yellow shade, and peered out. "So, ol' John Lewis escaped. He always swore he would."

"John?" I repeated. "So you knew him personally."

"We was partners."

"Partners?" I raised an eyebrow at Matt and Chace.

"In crime," Matt said under his breath.

Harlan looked at him sharply. "When I'm holding the gun, it ain't a good idea to start accusing people."

"But I thought you were the key witness against Torbett," I said, trying to get Harlan's attention away from Matt.

Harlan Cody turned back to peer out the window. "I was. Torbett done me wrong and I don't like it when people do that. So, I nailed him. I nailed him real good."

"You mean he didn't commit the murder?" Chace asked.

"No siree." Harlan slapped his knee and cackled with laughter. "That's some joke on him, ain't it?"

"Then you knew he was innocent?" I gasped.

"Of that murder? Sure. But he was guilty of lots of worse things." Harlan Cody rubbed the back of his neck. "And he knows it, too."

I was stunned. "How could you help put an innocent man in prison, knowing he would spend the rest of his life in a tiny cell?"

The old man blinked in surprise at me. "It was real easy."

"Can I have a drink of water?" Chace suddenly squeaked. "I'm kind of thirsty."

Chace started to move to the tiny kitchen at the back of the house but Harlan lifted his gun and growled, "Nobody goes anywhere until you tell me what you're doing mixed up with that varmint Torbett."

The sight of the gun in his face made Chace start talking a mile a minute. "We have nothing to do with Torbett. He said he was going to get revenge on the people who put him in prison and we wanted to warn you. But we probably shouldn't have bothered because it looks like you're the one who should be behind bars."

"Too late," Harlan retorted. "That murder happened fifty years ago." He hopped a little jig in a circle. "They'd never get me."

I realized we'd just heard *Harlan* confess that he had done the murder. Not Torbett. And he was dancing with glee.

"The statute of limitations never runs out on murder," Chace continued. "We could tell the police and have you arrested tomorrow."

I couldn't believe the words coming out of my brother's mouth. The last thing we needed was to get that strange little man angry at us — especially when he was holding a loaded shotgun. I tried to clap my hand across Chace's mouth.

At the same time Matt grabbed the cushion off the couch and threw it at Chace. "Put a cork in it, will you?"

The sudden movement from both of us startled Harlan and his finger must have pulled the trigger. A deafening boom erupted from the rifle and everyone jumped. Even Harlan.

We all stared up at the ceiling where a bullet had blown a hole in the plaster. Harlan looked down at his gun. "Darn thing. I never know when it's going to go off. Half the time it's jammed." He seemed to forget all about us as he broke the shotgun down and examined the barrel. "A feller could shoot his foot off, if he weren't careful."

As he continued muttering to himself, Matt, Chace, and I slowly backed toward the kitchen. Unfortunately, before we could reach the door a voice bellowed, "Harlan Cody! Let me in!"

Harlan nearly dropped his gun as J. L. Torbett kicked open the front door. His bulky frame filled the doorway and his red eyes glared at Harlan with an indescribably fierce hatred.

Harlan managed to put his shotgun back together and aimed it directly at his old enemy's massive chest. "Welcome back, you old skunk!"

I covered my eyes as another blast rocked the tiny room. J. L. Torbett grunted from the impact of the blast but didn't fall. As Harlan Cody struggled to reload his shotgun, Torbett lurched forward into the room.

"Revenge!" he moaned.

Before Harlan Cody could fire the gun again, Torbett grabbed him by the neck. The two of them crashed back and forth, knocking over the television set. That spurred Matt into action.

"Crawl!" he shouted, pointing toward the kitchen door. "And don't look back!"

"Get back, you rotted hunk of dog meat!" Harlan Cody warned. The horrible corpse just kept repeating, over and over again, "Revenge."

The three of us scurried through the tiny kitchen to the back door. Two shots had been fired and I was afraid that the next one would be aimed at us. Matt managed to get the door open just as the third blast went off.

We froze for a moment in the doorway and held our breaths. There was no sound at all coming from the living room. Just an awful stillness that seemed louder than the noise of the struggle.

I grabbed Matt by the arm and asked, "Do you think that shot hit Harlan?"

"I-I-I don't know," Matt stammered. "But I'm not sticking around to find out." Matt continued to stammer as he pointed behind me.

I turned and nearly fainted. J. L. Torbett stood swaying in the kitchen, clutching the shotgun. But what made me nearly pass out was the hole that had been blown open in the center of his chest. The orange prison coveralls were burnt black around the edges of the hole and I could see right through his body!

8

"Catch!" Matt shouted as he hurled a plastic bag of trash sitting by the back door at Torbett.

The sack caught the corpse squarely in the face and he staggered backwards into the living room. That was all the time we needed to make a break for it.

"Follow me!" Matt shouted.

We clattered down the dilapidated steps and sprinted out of the backyard. No sooner were we in the alley than the corpse burst through the back door with an enraged roar. "You'll pay for this!"

"He's still after us!" I shouted.

Matt led us straight toward a solid wooden fence and for a moment I thought he'd mistakenly led us into a corner. But he kicked the bottom of one of the boards and a section of the fence flipped up, leaving an opening wide enough to slip through. He held the board for Chace and me, barking, "Move it! He's right behind us."

I shoved Chace into the gap and, as soon as he was clear, scrambled after him. My knee scraped against something hard and sharp like a nail and the searing pain made me gasp. I almost felt relieved. Only moments before I was sure that I would never feel another thing.

Chace and I stumbled over each other as we splashed through the puddles in the alley. A crash of splintered wood came from behind us and I knew that Torbett had broken through the fence.

"Over there," Matt hissed, "to the right!"

This time we made for a narrow passage between an old corrugated tin shed and a wooden garage. We inched our way between the two buildings, then burst out onto a street. We were out in the open now. Matt sprinted ahead of us, veering from side to side in a zigzag pattern.

"Move like me," he urged. "You'll be harder to hit."

I didn't dare look behind me. I knew that if I saw that thing with its gruesome face, I wouldn't have been able to take another step. I could hear the dull *thunk-thunk* of his feet pounding down the pavement after us.

Suddenly Matt darted into an alley. An old red pickup truck blocked the way. Matt threw open the front door and shouted, "Get in!"

"No way!" I argued. "He'll find us." What sane person would get into a closed car knowing that a maniac with a shotgun was right behind them?

Matt shoved me into the truck. "I'm going to drive us out of here. Now get in."

"You can't drive this," I protested. "There's no key!"

"Yes, there is." Matt pushed me across the seat and Chace slid in next to me. Chace was craning his neck to look out the rear window.

Matt groped frantically under the dashboard with his hand muttering, "It was here yesterday."

"Let's go, Matt," Chace urged, staring anxiously out the rear window. "He's coming!"

"Got it!" Matt held up a key and slipped it into the ignition. The starter whirred but the engine didn't catch.

"What's the matter?" I demanded. "Why won't it go?"

"I don't know." Matt pounded the steering wheel with his fists. "Come on, you stupid piece of junk!"

The engine sputtered several times, then finally roared to life. With a screech of grinding metal, Matt slammed the car into gear.

"He's here!" Chace screamed.

The passenger door burst open just as we jerked forward. There was a sickening bump as the door slammed back and knocked Torbett to the ground.

"Take that, sucker," Matt said as he steered the truck down the alley. The three of us were jostled up and down like rag dolls as the truck hopped forward in fits and starts.

"Can't you go any faster?" Chace urged. "He's getting up off the ground."

"I don't know. We seem to be stuck in one gear." Matt tried to shift gears again but they made a terrible grinding sound.

"Oh, great," I muttered. "The one truck you choose to steal is a lemon."

"It's not a lemon," Matt said, pressing the gas pedal to the floor. The engine roared but we didn't seem to go any faster. "And it's not stolen. It belongs to my mother's boyfriend."

"We could walk faster than this," Chace complained. "Does it always drive like this?"

"I've never seen him drive it," Matt admitted. "He's usually just working on it."

My eyes widened. "You mean, this is a broken truck? Oh, this is great! This is just great! Listen to that." The engine was roaring so loudly that I had to shout to be heard. "We might as well have a loudspeaker announcing, 'Here we are, Torbett. Come and get us!' "

"You just keep an eye out for that thing," Matt shot back at me. He stared intently forward into the darkness, narrowly avoiding several parked cars that seemed to loom up in front of us out of nowhere. "I don't understand why I can't see any better."

"The headlights," I mumbled.

"What?" Matt jerked the wheel to avoid a green Dumpster and the truck bounced up onto the curb.

"The headlights," I repeated. "You forgot to turn them on."

"Oh." He flicked on the switch and the twin beams lit up the road in front of us.

"Is he still with us?" Matt asked, glancing nervously in the rearview mirror.

Chace shook his head. For the first time in what felt like an hour, I let out my breath. I leaned my head against the dashboard and murmured, "Thank goodness."

"I didn't know you knew how to drive," Chace said as the truck coughed and sputtered down the road.

"Brian — that's my mom's boyfriend — he lets me back his other car out of the driveway."

"No fair," Chace complained. "My dad won't even let me sit behind the wheel when the engine's running."

"Yeah, well, I'm still learning." Matt tried to shift gears again and he was answered once more by a shriek of metal. "I've never driven in any direction but reverse."

"Oh, that's terrific," I groaned. "Just terrific. If the police see you driving, they're going to stop you for sure."

"Who cares?" Chace replied. "Maybe we'll finally get their attention."

"I say we keep driving until this rotten town and that rotten corpse are a hundred miles behind us," Matt declared. He was gripping the steering wheel so hard that his knuckles were white.

"We can't!" I said, sitting bolt upright in my seat. "We've got to warn Gretchen."

In our close call with Torbett I'd forgotten all about my best friend. She was at the Keedy house with two children and had no idea that some horrible thing was stalking her. "Turn here," I ordered Matt.

"We'll stop at the next phone booth and try calling her again," Matt said, continuing to drive straight.

"There's no time for that," I said. "If Torbett's not following us, then he's on his way to the Keedys'. We've got to get there before he does."

Matt shot me a sideways look.

"Please, Matt," I said.

"Kelly's right," Chace added. "I think we have to go to the house."

I could see a small muscle twitching in Matt's jaw. He was upset but he did what we asked. With a swift turn of the wheel we made a U-turn and headed up Jackson Drive toward Mulberry Hill.

"If Harlan was the real murderer and not Torbett," I said, thinking out loud, "why would Torbett be trying to kill everyone?"

"Maybe all those years in jail turned him into a murderer," Matt said, still keeping his focus on the road. "Did you see the look of pure hate in his eyes? His mind could've just snapped."

"Besides, Harlan Cody said Torbett was guilty of lots of other crimes," Chace reminded me. "Crimes *worse* than murder."

"What could be worse than murder?" I asked.

"Torture," Chace answered. "I think that would be worse. Taking someone to the brink of death but letting them live."

I shuddered. "Stop it. That's making me sick."

"You're the one who asked."

"I didn't really want an answer," I retorted.

The truck hit the steepest part of the hill and smoke started pouring out from under the hood. Then a terrific backfire that sounded like a gunshot split the air and Chace let out a terrified howl that scared me worse than the noise. I dug my nails into Matt's knee and he yelped with pain, taking his foot off the gas. The truck bucked forward twice, then shuddered and died.

We were all embarrassed at our reactions to the backfire and for a few moments none of us said a thing. Finally Matt pushed open his door and said, "We'll have to run the rest of the way."

I didn't relish the idea of stepping out onto the street when Torbett could be out there waiting to grab us but we had no other choice. Chace and I clambered out after him and the three of us hurried up the hill, sticking to the center of the road.

"I think our wheels gave us a good head start

on him," Matt said. "But we can't be too careful."

Ahead of us the upper story of a large white colonial house peeked out above the crest of the hill. "There's the Keedy home."

It was a really nice house, with four wooden pillars along the front porch that stretched up to the eaves of the second floor. The porch lights were on and they sent long rectangular shadows across the manicured front lawn. Matt halted at the beginning of the driveway.

"Okay, go get your friend," he said. "Chace and I will keep watch out here."

I looked at the broad expanse of grass stretching between me and the porch light above the green front door. "What if he's watching?"

"Look, don't worry about being seen," Matt said. "Just worry about being fast. We don't have wheels anymore so we're going to have to get away from here on foot. Get Gretchen and those kids, and let's beat it out of here."

I put my head down and sprinted for all I was worth. I leapt onto the porch, hit the doorbell with the heel of my palm, and waited. No one came to the door. I peeked in the nearest window. The drapes were open and all the lights were on. I had a clear view of the den. Loud music was blasting from the television set and I figured Gretchen must be watching MTV. But the couch was empty. So were the armchairs. She wasn't sprawled out on the carpet, either. My heart started to beat a little harder and I prayed silently, "Please, don't let us be too late!"

I hit the doorbell again. And again. Finally I held my hand on it and counted to sixty. Still nothing. I raced back to the window and pounded on it, shouting, "*Gretchen!* Come to the door!"

A shadow moved in the kitchen and I froze in terror. The next thing I saw was the arm of a bright red and white sweater, and I gasped. That's what Gretchen had been wearing that day at school! I braced myself, afraid to think what might emerge from that door.

Then Gretchen strolled into the den, chatting away into a portable phone. She held a handful of popcorn and, after every other word, tossed a kernel into her mouth.

My relief turned to instant fury. "She's *still* on the *phone*? I don't believe it! *Gretchen!*"

By kicking up with my left foot, I could just reach the doorbell with my toe. I rang the bell with my foot and pounded on the window with my hand but she remained completely oblivious.

"Keep your voice down," a voice warned from beside me and I jumped back in alarm. It was Matt. "We can hear you all over the neighborhood."

"That stupid Gretchen is still blabbing on the phone," I explained. "The TV's blasting away, and she can't hear me knock or ring the bell."

"Did you try the door?" Matt asked, grasping the knob in his hand.

"Uh . . . I . . . well," I stammered, feeling too silly for not thinking of that first. Fortunately, Matt pulled back in disgust. "It's locked."

"So what do we do now?" I hissed.

Matt jumped off the porch and ran around the house trying to open the windows. They all were closed tight. Chace and I hurried after him and found Matt staring up at the second story. "We'll try to climb up that." He pointed to a rose trellis that ran up the side of the house. At the top of the trellis was what appeared to be a bathroom window. "It looks like that window's open."

Matt leapt in the air but the white wooden lattices were just out of his reach.

"Here, I'll give you a boost." Chace already had his fingers woven together in a makeshift step. I moved in beside Chace and urged. "Use my shoulder as another step."

It was weird. Only a few hours before, we couldn't manage to open a door together. Now we were working as a tight unit, trusting each other completely.

Matt braced his hands against the wall, put one foot in Chace's hands, and then put his other foot on my shoulder. When he pushed off, I nearly lost my balance but steadied myself long enough for Matt to catch hold of the trellis.

"You got it," Chace whispered as we watched Matt swing up onto the trellis and carefully work his way up the side of the wall. The window was just above his head to the right. He looked like Spiderman with his arms and legs spread out against the wall. Matt reached his right hand up above the ledge and caught hold of the top of the window frame. He gave it a push and called, "Hey, it's loose. If I could just get some leverage, I might be able to lift it up higher."

"Chace, let me stand on your shoulders," I said. "Then you can push off of my hands, Matt."

My brother quickly ducked down and lifted me up into the air. "You better hurry, Matt," Chace's muffled voice said from below me. "She weighs a ton."

At any other time I probably would have punched my brother for that comment but right then it didn't seem to matter. All I could think of was getting Matt in that window. That's probably why none of us heard the footsteps come up the drive behind us.

"What do you think you're doing?" a voice demanded from below.

Matt spun to see who was yelling and lost his balance. He tumbled down onto my shoulders and Chace collapsed under the weight of both of us. We hit the ground with a bone-jarring thud.

9

"I might have known it'd be you."

David Ensign stood with his hands on his hips above Matt. "I'm calling the police, Avery," he sneered, "and they'll put you in jail."

Matt had scraped his forehead during the fall and a streak of blood was running down one side of his face into his eye. He squinted up at David in confusion. "Wha-what are *you* doing here?"

"He's here to see Gretchen," Chace mumbled as he rolled out from under me. "What else?"

"Chace?" David's look of surprise turned to astonishment when I finally managed to sit up beside my brother. "And Kelly? All *three* of you are robbing this house?"

"No, you idiot!" I shouted in frustration. Every bruised and banged-up part of my body was starting to ache. The added humiliation of having David Ensign haughtily accuse us of being thieves made me furious. "Gretchen — who can't shut up on the phone long enough to even answer the doorbell —

is in danger. We're trying to get into the house to warn her."

"Danger?" David hooted with laughter. "Come on! You can do better than that."

Matt wiped the blood out of his eye with his T-shirt and leapt to his feet. "I'll show you how much better we can do!"

He slammed the palms of his hands into David's chest. The startled boy fell backwards onto the wet grass. Then Matt turned his back on David and said to me, "Let's try your friend one last time and then I'm getting out of here."

"Oh, no, you don't."

David scrambled to his feet and grabbed the back of Matt's jacket. He jerked Matt around and clipped him in the side of the head. Matt clapped his hand to his ear and howled in pain.

Before David could hit him again, Chace and I jumped him. I'd never hit anyone before (except maybe my brother when we were younger but that hardly counts) but after being so scared and helpless for so long that night, something clicked inside my head. We pummeled David with our fists in a blind rage. He cowered on the grass, shielding his head with his hands. "Stop! Stop!" he pleaded. "I give up."

Matt, who was the one who'd been hit by David in the first place, grabbed Chace and me by the back of our blue surgical gowns. "Calm down! Stop it, you two."

"What's going on out here?" I heard Gretchen's voice ask from the open front door. "David, is that you?"

How Gretchen, who was still clutching the phone, had managed to hear David's voice and not mine over the blare of the television, I'll never know. But there she was. And for the moment, it stopped the fight.

"Gretchen!" I bellowed. "Grab the Keedy kids, and get out of the house!"

She stared at me for a few seconds, then said into the phone, "Jenny, can I call you back? David's here."

I noticed how she didn't mention my name and then I realized why. The last time we had seen each other, we'd both said some awful things. She was still upset from our argument and knew nothing about J. L. Torbett, and the horrible murder he was about to commit. But how could she?

Gretchen pushed the antenna into the phone and stepped onto the porch. "What are you doing here?"

David peered out from behind his hands and, realizing no one was going to hit him anymore, stumbled to his feet. He raced to Gretchen's side and declared, "I caught these clowns trying to break into the house."

"What?" Gretchen gave me a nasty look. "Is this some pathetic attempt to get back at me?"

"You've got to believe us," I pleaded. "I know this looks weird but — "

"We'd better get inside," Matt cut in. He glanced nervously over his shoulder and whispered, "Something doesn't feel right."

I had the same sick feeling inside. That could only mean that Torbett was close by, maybe watching us from the shadows of the hedge. The image of the wild-eyed man with the gaping hole in his chest flashed through my head. "Gretchen, please, let's go in the house. There isn't much time to talk."

Maybe it was the sound of my voice or the way the three of us looked — torn clothes, bruised arms, haggard faces — but something convinced her to let us in the door.

We hurried into the hall and Matt instantly went into the living room and started pulling the drapes. "Chace, make sure the back door is locked."

"Got it." My brother hurried through the den and I heard the latch snap shut in the kitchen.

"Lock the front door," I told Gretchen as I flicked off the TV.

"Hey!" she protested. "I was watching that."

"We need to be able to hear." I moved to the foot of the stairs in the foyer. "Where are the kids? Upstairs?"

"Of course." Gretchen watched me in confusion. "They're asleep. Now will you tell me what this is all about?"

David, who was carefully checking a scrape on

his elbow, spat out, "I told you. I caught 'em trying to break into the house. Now they're just lying to cover up."

"David!" I barked. "Just *shut UP*!"

The frustrated anger in my voice caught him so by surprise that he actually staggered backwards a step. But he kept quiet. I knew we didn't have much time so I quickly turned to my friend and said in a low, urgent voice, "Gretchen, please forget what happened at school today. I'm sorry for whatever it was that I said."

"You called me a — "

"Just forget it, okay?" I barked. "Something so weird and terrible has happened that you probably won't believe me, but you have to. You *must*."

Chace and Matt stepped into the den from the kitchen. They looked like they had cleaned out the entire knife drawer. "Listen to Kelly," Matt urged. "She's telling the truth."

I decided against telling her the whole truth. I knew she wouldn't believe that. Instead I said, "A convict escaped this evening and hid at the mortuary."

"A convict?" David rolled his eyes. "Oh, puh-*leez*!"

"His name is J. L. Torbett," I continued, ignoring David. "He's been in prison for fifty years and he's sworn to get revenge on anyone who had anything to do with putting him in jail."

Gretchen narrowed her eyes suspiciously. "So? What's that got to do with me?"

"Nothing. Except that Judge Keedy was the judge who sentenced him. He's coming to this house tonight to get the judge. He's already visited two other people and he's attacking anyone or anything that gets in his way."

"But the judge isn't here," Gretchen said. "He's at that banquet with the Keedys."

I puffed out my cheeks in irritation. Sometimes my friend could be so dense. "I know that, Gretchen. And you know that. But Torbett doesn't. He's coming here right now."

"So we've got to get those kids, and get out of this house," Matt finished. "Now!"

Gretchen stared at me for a long time, and then crossed her arms. "How long did it take you three to come up with that story?"

Chace grabbed Gretchen by the shoulders and shook her. "It's not a story," he shouted. "Kelly's telling the truth. And this convict isn't just any convict, he's some kind of monster."

I heard Matt groan beside me. Once again my brother had said too much. "What do you think you're doing, Chace?" I shouted. "Now she'll never believe us."

"Well, it's the truth, Kelly," Chace shot back. "That thing's a walking corpse. You can't say it isn't so."

Gretchen's face hardened into a cold mask. "Kelly, this is not funny," she said in a clipped voice. "I'm in charge of those two kids. What if I really believed you and rushed out into the night with them? It'd scare them half to death. Then what would the Keedys think? They'd never hire me again."

Tears of frustration sprang to my eyes. The whole situation was impossible. "Look, Gretchen, if you have ever been my friend, please believe me."

Matt grabbed my arm. "It's no use. Let's get out of here."

I spun to face my friend once more. "Okay, Gretchen. If you insist on staying, would you do one thing for me? Call the police."

"And tell them what?"

"Tell them that you caught some prowlers trying to break in. Give them our names. I don't care. Tell them we were trying to rob you. Anything. Just get them to come here. You're going to need protection."

The color slowly drained out of Gretchen's face. "You really mean it, don't you?"

David nudged her with his elbow. "Don't fall for it."

I put my hand on my heart. "I have never been this serious in my entire life."

"But . . . but . . . how did you run into this

convict?" Gretchen sputtered. "I mean, how did he get into your house?"

Suddenly we heard a thud on the front porch.

"What was that?" Chace whispered.

Matt looked straight at me. "He's here."

"He?" David smirked. "Who else did you get to play this prank with you? Gretchen, these guys are just trying to pull a joke on you." He leaned forward and stuck his nose up close to my face. "But, hey, Halloween's over and we're not falling for it."

This time the handle rattled on the front door.

"Turn off the lights," Matt hissed.

Chace and I dove for the wall switches in the foyer, then raced around the house turning off the rest of the lights.

I grabbed the flashlight that I'd taken from the embalming room out of my pocket and, aiming the beam at the floor, hurried back to join the others in the den.

Matt was struggling with the couch, trying to shove it into the hall. "David, help me block the front door."

"No way. You're not going to make me look stupid."

"I don't have to make you look stupid," Matt hissed as Chace hurried over to help him. "You're doing fine on your own."

Gretchen was torn. She looked like she wanted to believe me but having David murmuring doubts in her ear was confusing. So she just stood in the hall, saying over and over, "Come on, is this a joke? Really, just tell me, Kelly. I promise I won't be mad anymore."

The scuffling sound was now at the den window. I knew he had to be standing just behind the drape. The porch light was still on and I could just make out the outline of his hulking shape. Gretchen saw it and marched over to the window. "Is Dutch Gleeson in on this, too?"

Dutch Gleeson is the biggest thug at Fairfield Middle School. Unfortunately, the outline in the window did look a whole lot like him. "Dutch," Gretchen shouted as she grabbed the edge of the curtain, "I am not impressed." Then with a flick of the wrist, Gretchen threw open the drape.

Pressed against the window was the most ghastly sight I have ever seen in my life. It was the same face, all right — the craggy features, haunted red eyes, and fierce hooked nose of J. L. Torbett. But something horrible was happening to his skin. The ashen pallor now had a greenish tinge. Open, festering sores were visible on his cheeks and forehead. His jaw hung open, revealing a hideously swollen black tongue. My hands flew to my mouth as I realized that the creature was decaying before our very eyes.

A wailing scream pierced the air. I knew it was coming not just from my throat but from every single person in that room.

10

"I think I'm going to be sick."

Gretchen clapped her hand over her mouth and stared at the window. The curtain was closed but we knew Torbett had to still be there.

"Gretchen, you better get a grip," Matt shouted as he raced for the hall closet and started throwing things out onto the floor. "It's only going to get worse."

"Did you see his face?" I hissed to Matt. "He's rotting."

"I've seen road kill that looked better." Matt held up a tennis racket and a fishing rod. "This might come in handy. Here, Kelly. Catch." He tossed the tennis racket to me and then started stringing the fishing line back and forth across the foyer to create a trip wire.

"Go tell that thing that the judge isn't here," Gretchen cried. "Tell it we have nothing to do with the Keedys."

"If its brain looks anything like its body, I don't

think it would understand that," Chace said, grabbing the fire irons from the fireplace.

The den window exploded in a crash of shattering glass and a heavy marble planter from the porch landed on the floor.

"He's breaking in!" Chace yelled.

"Upstairs!" I shouted. "Now!"

David was already pushing Gretchen up to the top of the landing. Chace and I clambered up after them, then watched breathlessly as Matt crisscrossed the fishing line between the banisters, all the way to the top of the stairs.

"That ought to slow him down," Matt said as he tied off the line. He slipped the coiled embalming tubes off his shoulder and looped the ends tightly around either side of the landing. "Go into the bedrooms," he told Chace, "and grab anything heavy. Bookends, paperweights, stuff like that."

Chace shook his head. "I don't understand."

"We need missiles for our slingshot," Matt explained. He pulled back on the tubing and let it go. It twanged like a bowstring. "If it worked for David against Goliath, why not for us?"

Chace broke into a grin. "Cool idea."

"Oh, no," Gretchen moaned. "He won't come upstairs, will he?"

A snarl answered her from the floor below as Torbett tripped over the wires in the den. He no longer sounded remotely human, but more like a rabid dog.

"The children," Gretchen suddenly gasped. "I've got to get them out of here."

"Is there a ladder or something?" I asked.

"There's a back stairway." Gretchen pointed to one of the doors at the end of the hall. "But it goes right past the kitchen."

I grabbed Matt's sleeve. "It's going to take time to get everyone out," I whispered. "Can you and Chace stall Torbett?"

Matt turned and our eyes met for a moment. The tiny night-light in the hall cast a soft glow that made his blue eyes gleam. A slight grin creased his face. "No sweat."

If I had ever doubted Matt before, it was gone forever. "Thanks, Matt," I murmured.

But Matt didn't hear me. His concentration was fixed totally on the rotting carcass downstairs. Torbett stumbled several times over the trip wires and snarled with frustration.

I turned back to Gretchen. "We'll keep that thing occupied while you and David get the kids out of here."

"What do we do when we get out?" David whispered.

"Run!" I hissed. "Run to your house. Call the police."

"But what about you?" Gretchen asked. "I can't just leave you here. Not after our fight in the lunchroom and everything. I feel just terrible. I mean, if I had known all of this was going to happen, I never would have said what I did."

I couldn't believe that Gretchen, the eternal motormouth, had picked this moment to launch into one of her long-winded apologies.

"I mean, you are my best friend," she continued, "and I'll never forget that you did this for me — "

"Gretchen!" I had to practically shout to get her to be quiet. "There isn't time for this. Let's just forget about our fight. Okay?"

Gretchen surprised me by keeping her reply short. "Okay." Then she hugged me and turned to David, "Come on, David, let's get Ruthie and Nathan and try not to wake them."

"If all the screaming that's been going on hasn't woken them up, then I don't think we have to worry," David muttered.

I watched the two of them tiptoe into the nursery, then made my way back down the hall to Matt and Chace. A tremendous crash came from downstairs. "What was that?" I demanded.

Chace grinned. "Matt's trip wires are working great. That thing still can't get up the stairs."

I watched Matt lean over the railing. He pointed something at the den and there was suddenly a flash of light and screech of sound. Matt had clicked on the television with the remote control.

The corpse was so startled by the sound that it actually jumped backwards. Then Torbett lunged into the den and slammed the television off its cart with a swipe of his hand. The picture tube exploded with a terrific bang.

In the nursery I could hear the whimpering protests of Nathan as Gretchen hurriedly wrapped him in a blanket and slipped him into a baby backpack. David and Gretchen reappeared in the hall and then made their way to Ruthie's room.

In the meantime, Matt and Chace were launching whatever they could grab with their makeshift slingshot. When Chace gave him a metal alarm clock, Matt turned to me and grinned. "Want to see time fly?" He pulled back on the tubing with all his weight and let it go.

Chace handed him a bathroom scale and Matt flung it like a Frisbee. A second later a howl came from downstairs.

"Bull's-eye!" Chace cheered.

Gretchen and David came running back into the hall. Nathan was sleeping soundly in the baby pack on her back while David held Ruthie on his shoulder. "We're ready," Gretchen said.

"Once you reach your house," I said, "get your parents to go to that banquet and tell the Keedys not to come home."

David nodded. "Got it."

"And use the phone *only* to call the police," I added. "I want to be able to reach you."

"What do you think I'm going to do, start calling

all the kids in Fairfield?" Gretchen asked defensively.

"Yes," I shot back. "I know you. Once you start dialing numbers, you can't stop. I think it's an addiction."

"Oh, Kelly, that's not true."

"It is," David cut in. "You were on the phone all night. I couldn't get through to you."

"See?" I put my hands on my hips and chided, "If you hadn't been on the phone, I could have warned you. Then you would have been safely out of here and would never have had to worry about a monster tearing the living room apart while you tried to sneak down the back stairs."

Gretchen's eyes glistened in the dim light of the hallway. "Oh, Kelly, I'm really scared."

I took a deep breath. "We're all scared but you can't think about that. Just think about Ruthie and Nathan. Now head for those stairs and don't look back."

"Kelly, I don't want to leave you," she said. "You're my best friend."

It felt really good to hear Gretchen say that. At that moment, when it seemed as if the whole world had gone crazy, I realized how much I needed her friendship.

"You're mine, too," I murmured. "And if you want to stay that way, get back to your house now."

"But what about Matt?" David asked. "Shouldn't we help him?"

Only an hour before, David had been threatening to beat Matt up and turn him over to the police. Now he seemed to really care about him.

"Chace and I will do that," I said, hoping my voice had more confidence than I felt. I gave Gretchen and David a gentle shove. "You've got to get Ruthie and Nathan someplace safe. Now go!"

"And call the police," Chace added. "Call the National Guard. Call anybody."

"*Arrghhh!*" Torbett's howl cut through the air as a crash sounded from downstairs.

"Run for it!" I shouted.

That was all the encouragement they needed. I watched Gretchen and David disappear down the stairs with the kids into the darkness and I felt a wistful tightness in my throat. I hoped I'd see them again. Soon. I shook my head, trying to get that awful thought out of my mind.

Suddenly there was a deathly stillness on the floor below. "Kelly," Matt hissed. "Hand me your flashlight."

"What are you going to do with it?" I asked as I pressed it into his palm.

"Watch." Matt tied some fishing line around the plastic casing, then flicked on the beam. He slowly lowered the flashlight over the railing to the level below. "We've got to keep his attention on us."

I peered over the banister and watched as Matt moved the light back and forth in the darkness. It really did look like someone was walking around downstairs with a flashlight. It must have convinced Torbett because we heard a mighty roar as he dove for the light. It swung wildly back and forth. Matt took several steps down the stairs as he reeled the light out of Torbett's reach. "Kelly, you and Chace take the back stairs and get out of here," he called back over his shoulder. "Now!"

We didn't question his order but raced for the stairs. They led into the kitchen, where we sprinted for the back door and made our way out into the night. Only then did we stop to catch our breaths. I turned toward the house, expecting to see Matt standing beside us. But there was no one there.

"Didn't Matt come out with us?" I asked.

Chace shrugged helplessly. "I thought he was right behind me."

I could see through the window into the living room. It was completely dark inside the house except for a single beam of light. It had to be Matt's flashlight. I watched the light move across the room and then freeze.

"Matt, don't be stupid," I murmured. "Torbett won't fall for that trick again. Get out of there."

My worst fears were confirmed when the light jerked violently and then went out. A horrible shriek filled the air.

"Oh, my God," Chace moaned. "He got Matt."

"What should we do?" I asked, wringing my hands helplessly. "Should we go in and try to help him?"

"No way," Chace said, backing away. "That thing'll just nail us, too."

I slumped down onto the damp grass. "Poor Matt! Torbett probably ripped him to shreds."

"That slice of road pizza never laid a hand on me," a voice called from the kitchen door.

"Matt?" I gasped. "But I saw the light and heard you scream."

Matt kicked open the back screen and leaned heavily against the door frame. He looked drained and exhausted. "Before we went upstairs I opened the door to the basement. While you guys were escaping I used the flashlight to lure him to the open door. When he swung at the flashlight he fell into the basement. The shriek you heard was him hitting the concrete."

"You mean, that, that *thing* is in the basement?" Chace stared at the tiny windows along the foundation and hurriedly backed away.

Matt nodded his head. "But I don't think he'll bother us anymore. I saw him at the bottom of the stairs. He was just lying there very still. It looked like his neck was broken from the fall."

"Did you lock the basement door?" I asked, as I instinctively inched backwards.

Matt rubbed his eyes with his hands. "Why should I? He's dead."

A terrible fear crept up my back like a giant spider. "But, Matt," I murmured as something rustled inside the house, "Torbett was already dead."

11

"Matt!" Chace shouted. "Behind you."

A hand exploded through the glass door and caught hold of the collar of Matt's leather jacket. He wriggled desperately but was pinned against the door.

"Your jacket," I shouted. "Take it off."

In a flash Matt slipped out of the arms of his jacket and scrambled on his hands and knees across the grass.

John Torbett — or what was left of him — lurched through the back door and I gasped in horror. His face and hands were decaying at an incredible speed. The gaping hole in his chest made it hard to see how he could stand up. His head drooped weirdly toward his right shoulder. Only the red eyes held anything resembling a spark of life — but the light burning there was so full of hate that I had to turn my head away.

"Kelly," Matt shouted. "Get out of here!"

I raced across the vast lawn toward a little iron

gate leading out the back of the hedge. My sudden movement caught Torbett's attention and he let out a loud roar.

"The gate's locked," I yelled as I struggled with the latch. "I can't seem to get it open."

Torbett lurched toward me.

"Hey, slime ball!" Matt shouted. He pulled up a flagstone from the garden path and flung it like a discus at the corpse. "Over here."

The rock thunked against the corpse's back and fell to the ground. Torbett spun around and the sight of his head flopping back and forth made me sick. He changed direction and staggered for Matt, who backed toward the side of the house.

"What are you doing, Matt?" Chace choked out. "Now he's coming after you."

"That's the idea," Matt said. "I want to keep him from following Kelly. You guys make a break for it."

"And what will you do then?" I yelled.

"I don't know," he called. "I'll figure something out."

Matt led Torbett in a wide circle around the yard, taunting him constantly. "I'm over here, no-neck! Try and catch me!"

Matt managed to lead Torbett to the edge of the Keedys' swimming pool that was covered up for the winter. Matt was so busy hopping up and down and screaming at the corpse that he didn't realize he was backing himself into a corner between the pool and the utility shed.

"He's boxed himself in," I cried.

"I'll get him!" Chace skirted the edge of the pool and grabbed an aluminum pole hanging from a pair of hooks on the side of the little house. The pole was about twelve feet long and had a skimming net at one end.

"Aieeee!" Chace charged the corpse and looped the net down over the monster's head. I ran in beside Chace and together we tugged Torbett away from Matt. The netting wasn't that big or strong but it was just enough to throw the corpse off-balance. He flailed his arms out to the side as he stumbled backwards.

"Into the pool!" Matt yelled.

Chace and I jerked the pole with all our might, as Matt dashed in and shoved the creature. The net broke off the end of the pole and Torbett toppled onto the plastic tarp covering the pool.

Then Matt started unhooking the pool cover from its pinnings. I realized what he was up to and told Chace, "Do whatever you have to do to keep that thing on the tarp." I ran to the opposite side of the pool and began releasing the metal latches holding the pool cover down.

Luckily there was still a lot of water under the tarp and the corpse couldn't manage to get to his feet. He flailed wildly, his head still caught in the net. Everytime he seemed about to free himself,

Chace would push him down with the end of the aluminum pole.

"Let's roll him up like a carpet," I shouted once we'd loosed all the ties.

"Just what I was thinking," Matt called back.

We looped the tarp over the body that was growling and struggling to stand and towed him into the shallow end of the pool. Matt's foot slipped and he suddenly plunged into the icy water.

"Are you okay?" I called.

"I'm fine," Matt yelled as he sloshed through the shallow water. "Now let's get him over the edge onto the ground."

Chace and I were straining with all our might but it was no use. "We can't," I said. "He's too heavy."

Matt, gasping from the cold, waded up behind the body wrapped in plastic. "Here, I'll push."

"Get out of the water, Matt," I said, tugging on the heavy tarp. "You'll freeze to death."

Matt pressed his shoulder up against the corpse, then yelled, "On the count of three, okay? One. Two. *Three*!"

Between the three of us we half pulled, half dragged the groaning corpse out of the pool. Matt pulled himself out of the water and helped us shove Torbett onto the grass in front of the utility shed. The cold water must have subdued the corpse because he was hardly struggling. I was grateful to have a chance to catch my breath.

"We're going to have to find a rope or something to keep him tied down," Matt said. His teeth were chattering so badly that he could barely get his words out. "For a rotting old carcass he sure is strong."

I noticed several garden hoses coiled by the door to the shed. "What about those?" I suggested.

"Great idea," Chace said. He jumped up and unscrewed one end from the faucet, then dragged the green tubing over to us. Matt wrapped one end of the hose around the sheath of plastic encasing the body, and handed me the other end.

"Here, loop this around him," Matt said. "Chace, you start at the other end." He glanced over his shoulder at the utility shed. "I'm going to see if there's anything else we can use in there. Be right back."

Chace and I set to work with a vengeance. We were about half done when the corpse started rolling around inside the plastic. "Matt?" I called. "We need help out here."

I was answered by several loud crashes that sounded like tin cans being knocked over.

"Better get back here pronto," Chace yelled, "or else we're going to have one loose monster on our hands."

Matt threw open the doors of the shed and appeared with a long length of heavy metal chain.

While Chace and I knotted the hose over and over, Matt wrapped the chain around our package and secured it with a padlock at one end. The corpse stopped struggling again and we sat back on our heels.

"Now that we've got him tied up," Chace wondered out loud, "what are we going to do with him?"

"I say, leave him here and let the police deal with him," I suggested. "Hopefully Gretchen has called them by now."

Matt shook his head. "You know we can't do that, Kelly. If he manages to escape, then he'll be after you two. Don't forget he knows where you live."

I knew Matt was right. The lump at our feet was motionless but that didn't mean it was no longer dangerous. I shivered in the dark.

"But what are we going to do?" I whispered so the monster couldn't hear me. "We already know you can't kill him."

"Yeah, but you *can* wound him," Chace pointed out. "I mean, he's not regenerating, or anything like that."

"What we need to do," Matt said slowly, "is turn him into nothing. Vaporize him."

"Vaporize him?" I repeated. "With what? Our laser guns?"

Matt chuckled, slightly embarrassed. "I guess I've been watching too many sci-fi movies."

"I know this sounds stupid," Chace said. "But why don't we take him to our house. That way we'll know where he is and then Dad can help us figure out what to do with this guy."

"It's not a stupid idea," Matt said, clapping Chace on the shoulder. "I think it's the only thing we can do."

"I hate to be a party pooper," I said. "But how are we going to get him there? The truck's broken down. Our bikes are at Harlan's. We certainly can't carry him."

Without a word Matt jumped up and ran into the shed.

"Hey, I'm not finished yet," I yelled. "Then there's the problem of — "

The roar of an engine erupted from inside the shed. Then the glare of two headlights hit us square in the eyes.

"What's that?" I said, squinting into the light.

A small green machine that looked like a miniature tractor rumbled out onto the lawn.

"It's a power mower," Chace cried with glee. "Matt, you are brilliant!"

12

The tractor mower had an aluminum trash cart hitched behind it. Matt backed the trailer up to the corpse and we attempted to maneuver it into the cart. It took us several minutes but we finally managed to slide the blue tarpaulin and its terrible contents in place.

Matt sat in the driver's seat while Chace and I perched on top of the metal shield covering the metal mowing blade. It made a perfect running board on either side of the tractor.

"This is great," Matt said, fiddling with a pair of levers attached to the steering column. "No gears to shift. You just put it in forward, and away we go." He pushed the lever forward and I could feel the spinning of the mowing blade vibrate beneath the shield.

"Whoa!" Chace shouted as he and I leapt back onto the ground. "Turn it off, dude."

Matt gave me a sheepish grin as he stopped the mower blade. "Sorry. I've got it now."

I narrowed my eyes at him suspiciously. "You sure?"

"Positive."

I gingerly climbed back on and this time we eased forward with just the engine humming and moved down the driveway toward the road.

"Hey, this is kind of fun," Chace announced as we putted along at no more than five miles an hour down the ridged road of Mulberry Hill.

I smiled for what felt like the first time in days. "If this whole terrible night hadn't happened, and if we weren't towing a monster in a trash cart, I'd say it was tons of fun."

We crested the hill and the twinkling lights of Fairfield spread out below us in the quiet night.

"All of those people are sleeping safely in their homes," Matt said softly. "They have no idea what's been going on in their own backyards and alleys."

The night breeze made my hair stream out behind me. The crisp air felt good. I gave my head a shake and took a deep breath. "It's like we've spent a night in a whole other world. One without parents or teachers — "

"Or cops," Matt added with a laugh. "They've probably been hanging out at Bud's Café, drinking coffee and scarfing doughnuts."

Chace chuckled at the thought. "Some crackerjack police force we've got. Remind me to call the Marines next time this happens."

"Next time," I repeated with a shudder. "Don't even kid about that, Chace. It's not funny at all."

At the bottom of the hill Matt slowed for the stop sign. No cars were in sight so he cruised straight through to Jackson Drive.

"I don't know about you guys," Matt declared, "but I want this to be my one and only experience with the other side."

He shivered violently and I realized he was still soaked from the swimming pool. His clothes must have felt like ice cubes against his skin. I was still wearing one of my dad's blue surgical gowns from the embalming room. As we rode along I slipped out of it and wrapped it around Matt's shaking shoulders.

"Here," I said. "It isn't much, but it might make you feel a little warmer."

"Thanks, Kelly." Matt shot me a glance out of the corner of his eye and smiled. "You know, you're all right."

I'm glad it was dark because I could feel my cheeks heating up. I knew the tips of my ears were blazing a bright red. "You're not so bad yourself," I murmured back.

It was weird. Earlier that evening the thought of spending more than ten minutes in a room with Matt Avery would have seemed like agony. Now the idea of spending ten minutes away from him felt far worse.

"Hey!" Chace leaned over and stuck his face in front of Matt. "What about me?"

"You?" Matt chuckled. "You're squid bait."

"Squid bait!" Chace repeated indignantly. "What kind of a name is that?"

"It's perfect," I giggled. "I only wish I'd thought of it."

"I was only kidding." Matt reached out his left hand and ruffled Chace's hair. "Hey, you hang with me so you must be cool."

The honk of a car horn blasted from behind us. I looked over my shoulder just as a car sped past. Someone leaned out the passenger window and yelled, "Get off the road, you idiots!" The car cut back sharply in front of us and Matt had to swerve hard to the right to avoid hitting the rear of the car.

"Hang on," he shouted as the tractor wobbled wildly on two wheels. I barely kept from being thrown off by grabbing Matt's sleeve. In a heart-beat it was over and we were alone on the road again.

"You guys okay?" I asked as we drove along in silence.

"Yeah, I think so," Chace said weakly.

"That jerk," Matt muttered under his breath. "He could see me. I've got my headlights on."

"That's the first car we've seen this evening," I mused as we rode past row after row of quiet houses. The tree-lined streets were peaceful and calm. Only the *put-put* of the mower engine broke the stillness.

"It's strange, isn't it?" Chace said. "It reminds me of that old TV show, *The Twilight Zone*. Have you seen any of those tapes?"

Matt nodded. "Yeah. It's like we've spent the evening in another dimension and have now slipped back into our own world."

"Only on the TV shows the horrible gruesome body stays behind in its own dimension," I reminded them. I turned to gesture back at the trash cart. "While we've brought ours with . . . oh, *no*!"

"What?" Matt slammed on the brakes of the tractor mower, practically sending me and Chace over the hood. "What's the matter?"

"Look behind us." I hung my head in my hands and moaned, "He's gone."

The little cart that we had been towing was still hitched to the tractor but the body was gone. The blue plastic tarpaulin, the heavy metal chains, the green garden hose — all of it had vanished.

Matt leapt off the mower and stood looking behind us into the dark. "We must have lost him when I swerved to avoid that car."

"Then we'd better go back and get him," Chace said. He took the wheel and started to turn the tractor around.

"No!" I gasped. "Let's just leave him. We've done enough. Someone else can find him and someone else can dispose of him. Oh, please!"

"Wait a minute, Kelly." Matt faced me with his hands on his hips. "What if he gets loose?"

"He's wrapped up in a ton of that plastic stuff," Chace reminded him. "Plus he's tied up with chains and about a hundred feet of garden hose. How could he break out of that?"

"Besides, how do we know he fell off just now?" I asked. "I didn't hear anything, did you?"

Both boys shook their heads.

"He could have fallen off anywhere," I said. "When was the last time you checked to see if he was on the cart?"

"Not since we started out," Matt admitted. "I was concentrating on my driving."

"Oh, please, you guys. We were having such a good time when we weren't thinking about him. Let's just go on the way we were."

Matt still wasn't convinced. He stared vainly back in the direction we'd come, hoping to catch a glimpse of where we'd lost Torbett.

"Maybe Kelly's right," Chace said. "We've done our part. We tried to warn Harlan and Clara. We saved Gretchen and the kids. We've done enough."

I got off the mower and grabbed Matt's arm. "Let's just go back to our house." My voice brightened as I added, "Maybe Mom and Dad are home. We can tell them all about it."

"Yeah," Chace said with a laugh. "They'll never believe us."

"They will when they get a look at the hole in the wall of the prep room," said Matt.

I shook my head in frustration. "Oh, Chace, it won't matter what they think. I can't take any more of this." My voice cracked in my throat and I finished miserably, "I just want to go home."

Matt took one long searching look into the darkness. Nothing moved. Nothing stirred. Finally he turned and, hopping back onto the mower, started the engine. "If that's what you want, Kelly."

I hopped on the running board beside him. "It's definitely what I want. Now, please — let's get out of here."

13

Anderson Mortuary was shrouded in darkness. The dark glass of the windows from upstairs reflected the light from the lone street lamp on the corner. For a moment I imagined the building had eyes and was watching us. We stood on the sidewalk and stared up at the massive building.

"Should we go inside?" Chace asked softly.

"Of course," I replied. "It's our home, isn't it?"

Home didn't seem to be the right word for the place at all. Tonight with all the lights out, it looked more like a vast tomb. Chace pushed open the front door, which was unlocked, and we stepped into the front entrance hall. Looking through the chapel I could just make out a faint red glow above the door to the embalming room, the same warning light that had set the stage for the entire disastrous evening.

Chace flicked a few of the light switches just inside the door and the brass-and-glass fixture in the hall glowed above our heads. A soft amber light came from the chandelier in the chapel.

"I was really hoping that Mom and Dad would be home," Chace said suddenly. "I mean, I *really* wished for that."

"Me, too." I looked at the hands on the old grandfather clock. "It's almost eleven. Where could they be?"

The front door shut loudly behind us and Chace and I jumped in alarm. We spun around to see Matt locking the heavy wooden door. "I think it's time for less talk and more action," he said. "Don't forget that thing is still out there and you guys have a giant hole in the side of your building."

"The embalming room," I gasped. "I forgot all about that window."

Chace was already moving down the hall. "Come on, Matt. We need to board that up now!"

Matt caught hold of Chace's arm. "Not so fast. We need things to work with. Do you have any wood?"

"Do we have any wood?" Chace giggled. "Our entire basement is filled with wooden coffins."

"Teak, oak, maple, pine, cherry. You name it," I said. "We've got the box."

"We don't really need a fancy box," Matt said.

"How about a shipping crate?" I suggested.

"Shipping?" Matt repeated. "You ship bodies?"

"Sure," Chace said with a shrug. "Some people send flowers, we send stiffs."

"Sometimes people die while they're away on

vacation," I explained. "Or they want to be buried in their hometown. That's when we put them in wooden crates and ship them."

Chace nodded. "A couple of those crates would be perfect for blocking the window."

"Then what are we waiting for?" Matt asked. "Let's grab one."

"They're down in the basement." Chace motioned toward the stairs and I watched the boys hurry away without me.

"Wait a minute!" I cried. "Don't leave me here all alone."

"Then come with us," Chace called back over his shoulder.

I really hate going down in the basement. Almost more than going into the prep room. Something about it terrifies me.

"I . . . I can't go down there," I murmured.

Matt came back and took me by the arm. He led me into one of the back pews of our little chapel. The chandelier twinkled warmly overhead. "Why don't you sit here, Kelly? From here, you can watch the front door, the basement door, and the corridor leading to the preparation room. You'll be safe."

I flopped down on the wooden bench. "Are you sure?"

Matt nodded. "And if anything strange happens, just sing out. Chace and I will be up those stairs in a flash."

"Okay," I said. "But be careful."

"Careful is my middle name." Matt squeezed my hand and then jogged back to the stairs. At the top step he cupped his hand around his mouth and shouted, "Chace, you down there?"

"Yes, I'm down here," an irritated voice answered. "And I just got a hernia trying to lift this thing by myself."

Matt turned back to me and held his arms out to the sides. "See? We can hear plain as day. Be right back."

I watched Matt disappear down the stairs and then sat very still, listening. I could hear the boys shouting at each other and loud clunking sounds as they tried to move the wooden coffins around. Then I focused on the smaller sounds. The ticking of the clock in the front entryway. The hum of the lights above my head. I listened to my own breathing, and the soft rustling of my pants against the wooden pew. I ducked my head down and stared at my feet. That's when I felt it.

There was no sound and nothing I could actually see. But I could sense it as clearly as if it were a loud siren or a spotlight. There was a body in the building. And not just in the building, but in the room with me. I knew it. The goose bumps started at my feet and traveled to the roots of my hair.

It took every ounce of courage I had to lift my head. I stared at the altar in front of me. It was draped in crisp white linen. A brass cross gleamed in the light. The empty podium was just to the right. Behind that was the little alcove reserved for family members who didn't want other mourners to see them. A flimsy gauze curtain was draped across the entrance.

I stared hard at the transparent curtain, waiting for a sound or a movement to give him away. The clock ticked. The lights hummed. My heart pounded louder than ever before. It was so loud that I was afraid I wouldn't be able to hear him when he came for me. And I knew he would come.

I scanned the room once more, searching the corners for the dreaded corpse. Once again my eyes came to rest on the curtain. And that's when I saw it.

Out of the shadows two red dots burned like the tips of fiery pokers. They were staring right at me.

14

"You," I said in a low, shaky voice. "Whatever you are, or have become — stay away from me. You hear?"

It didn't answer. Those ghastly red eyes never wavered or blinked but stared at me as if trying to burn a hole in my skull. I felt a deep tightness in my throat like I was being smothered. Then the gauze curtain rustled and the corpse emerged.

It no longer even resembled the man called Torbett. Beneath the tattered orange prison uniform was a skeleton with ragged fragments of skin clinging to its exposed bones. The jaws chewed soundlessly like rusty hinges. The long bony fingers made clicking sounds as they clutched and grasped the air.

I wanted to get up and run but I couldn't make my legs move. Panic rose in my throat threatening to drown me in fear. All I could do was watch helplessly as the body lurched closer and closer.

I opened my mouth and a blood-curdling scream

filled the room. I screamed as I stumbled to my feet. I screamed as I knocked a planter resting on a stone pedestal by the door onto the floor. I screamed as I ran toward the embalming room. My voice was hoarse from screaming but I couldn't stop.

The thing followed me into the hall, its eyes glowing like two red searchlights, never letting me out of their beams.

I grabbed the door of the embalming room and twisted the knob. It wouldn't budge. Then I remembered that Torbett had locked the dead bolt and taken the key.

"Matt! Chace!" I shrieked as loudly as I could. "Help!"

The corpse followed me as I pounded down the corridor to the elevator. Praying that the car wasn't in the basement, I hit the call button. The elevator's engine rumbled to life. "Hurry!" I pleaded. "Hurry!"

The shredded remains of Torbett lunged forward just as the doors parted. Matt and Chace stood inside the car, supporting an open plywood casket between them. They must not have heard my screams because Chace was grinning broadly, as he cracked, "First floor. Lingerie!"

The smile instantly disappeared when he saw what was behind me. "Look out!"

Matt grabbed my arm and yanked me into the elevator, shouting, "Close the door!"

Chace hit the button but it was too late. Torbett lurched into the car just before the doors closed. I clung to Matt, trying to keep as far away from the rotting skeleton as possible.

"Do something!" Chace howled.

Matt still had one hand on the wooden coffin. He jammed it forward, pinning the remains of Torbett against the elevator doors. All three of us threw our weight against the back of the box and for a moment we had him trapped inside like a fly in a bottle.

"What do we do next?" I gasped. "The elevator doors are going to open and he'll escape."

Matt watched the dial over the door, the muscle twitching in his jaw. As the elevator came to a stop and the doors opened into the sub basement, Matt pushed his back against the wall of the elevator and shoved outward with all of his strength. The thing fell backwards onto the concrete with the plywood crate still on top of it.

Chace and Matt quickly leapt on the coffin, using their weight to keep Torbett's skeleton pinned down.

We were in the tiny concrete room housing the crematory. The retort, a giant gas oven made of steel and lined with firebrick like a kiln, stood only a few yards from us.

"Kelly, switch on the main burner," Chace called as he struggled to hold down the casket. "There's only one thing left to do. We'll nuke him in the oven." The box hopped up and down, tossing the boys from side to side like a bucking bronco, as the monster struggled to free itself.

I raced to the control panel by the side of the oven. Two rows of red and blue buttons sat beneath a giant temperature gauge. "We have to run the exhaust fan first," I said. "That'll take at least five minutes."

"Exhaust fan!" Matt's voice reflected the jolting that was happening to his entire body. "Forget that, and hit the gas. We can't hold him much longer."

I ran my hand over my face in frustration. "But Dad told me that there is usually residual gas in the chimney. If we don't flush it out with the exhaust fan, it could explode and blow us sky high."

"Like it really matters?" Matt choked. "This thing is about to break loose. I think I'd rather be launched than have to deal with him."

"Kelly!" Chace screamed desperately. "Hit the main burners *now*!"

I shut my eyes and punched the red button. The gas jets ignited with a whoosh. The temperature dial was already set for normal burning — 2200°.

"Open the oven door," Matt shouted.

I grabbed a handle of the massive metal door, which was four feet square, and pulled it open. The blast of heat from inside singed my eyebrows and eyelids. I leaped back, shouting, "Push him in. Now."

I was answered by a loud roar. When I spun around I saw the skeleton had gotten up from the concrete floor. His bony arms held the plywood coffin, with Chace and Matt still clinging to the top, above his head. He tossed them and the coffin against the far wall as if they were irritating flies. He didn't even give them a backward glance but turned toward me.

"No . . . one . . ." The voice drooped and moaned like a tape player with batteries that were running down. "No . . . one . . . gets . . . in . . . my . . . way."

It moved forward and I instinctively took a step backwards, then gasped with pain. The searing heat of the open oven stung my back right through my clothes. I knew that if I retreated any further, I'd be horribly burned. But there was no where else to go. The crematory room had deliberately been sealed with no windows to protect the rest of the house from any accidental fire. The elevator and stairway were both behind the skeleton. I was caught.

"Matt! Chace!" I moaned. "Help . . ."

The plea died in my throat as I looked over at them. Both boys had been dazed by their fall against the cement wall. Chace lay completely stunned, his eyes unable to focus on anything. Matt rose to his knees unsteadily, then slipped back to the ground. The cut on his forehead had burst open and his face was covered with blood.

I knew they could do nothing for me now. The terrible monster had won.

With his arms extended in front of him, Torbett dove for me.

"Duck!" Matt shouted.

I fell to my knees as the decayed corpse hurtled over my head right into the oven.

"Die, sucker!" Matt yelled as he swung the heavy steel door shut.

A howl came from inside the oven that sounded like nothing of this earth. It rose in pitch like a siren, growing louder and louder until I thought my eardrums would burst. We clapped our hands over our ears and tried to keep out the sound.

Then suddenly it was over. I could feel it. The evil that had tormented us was gone.

15

"Kelly?"

My mother's voice echoed down the stairwell into the crematory.

"Chace! Where are you?"

My brother and I were sitting on the floor, our backs pressed against the elevator doors, staring glassy-eyed at the oven in front of us. Matt lay on his back, looking up at the ceiling. I don't know how long we had been in that position. It seemed like hours.

I struggled to my feet and opened the door into the stairwell. "We're down here, mother." My voice was so hoarse from all my screaming that I could barely croak. "In the crematory."

"What are you doing down there?" she called. "You know that place is dangerous. It's absolutely off-limits. Get up here this minute."

Chace and Matt both stood up. Matt rubbed his shoulder and winced. Chace shuffled over to the control panel and pressed a blue button. The roar of the gas jets in the oven diminished into a soft breeze, then stopped completely. Matt opened the elevator doors and stepped into the car.

"We're going to have to tell her," I said. "Once she sees the broken window in the embalming room she'll want to know what's been going on."

Chace nodded wearily. "I know. But how?"

Matt, who was holding the door for us, said, "Start at the beginning, and when we get to the end — stop."

I chuckled and shook my head. "She probably won't believe us, but it doesn't really matter."

"That's right," Chace murmured. "We know it happened. And we know we survived."

"Survived," I repeated in a whisper.

We shared this one last moment together in silence.

Finally Chace gestured upstairs with his thumb, where we could hear my mother talking to my father, and said, "Shall we face the music?"

"Let's do it," Matt said.

My mother was standing in the foyer talking on the phone when the elevator doors opened. From the tone of her voice I knew it had to be her sister on the other end. "What a horrendous night," she was saying. "The banquet was a disaster, the food didn't arrive till nearly nine, and just as Arthur was supposed to give his speech, his beeper went off. We had to skip dinner and the speech and leave on an urgent death call."

"A death call?" Chace whispered as we stepped into the shadows of the chapel. "Who do you think it could be?"

Matt shook his head. "Clara Simpson. Maybe Harlan Cody. We never really found out what happened to either of them."

"We had to drive all the way out to Brinkman," my mother continued into the phone.

"Brinkman?" Matt repeated. "Isn't that the state prison?"

Chace nodded. "You don't think *another* prisoner — "

I suddenly gasped, cutting off my brother in mid-sentence. I was getting that awful feeling again. Goose bumps raced up my arms and legs.

"It's here," I whispered. "In the building."

Matt stared hard at my face. "What is?"

"A body. I can feel it."

Chace nudged Matt and pointed to the door that led to the garage. It was ajar and the sound of a car could be heard through it. "Kelly's right. Dad just pulled into the garage."

"You don't mind if I miss this?" Matt said with a weak smile. "I think I've seen enough bodies to last a lifetime."

"Sorry," I said, putting my hand on his arm. "But you're going to have to see another one. There's no way to avoid it in this house."

"Dad's bringing it in now," Chace said.

We heard the squeak of wheels and then a sharp

bump as the edge of the gurney knocked open the door from the garage. A pair of feet with a tag hanging from the left toe appeared, followed by the rest of the body covered in a white shroud.

"Oh, listen, Millie," my mother said into the phone, "I've got to go. Arthur's bringing in the customer." She sighed and said, "It's going to be another long night. I'll talk to you tomorrow."

Chace grabbed my arm and squeezed it till I thought he would break the bone.

"What is it?" I demanded. "You're hurting me."

He whispered, "Look at the toes."

Matt had turned his head away to avoid looking at the body. He looked up and his eyes grew huge as he recognized the purple veins and yellowed nails of the corpse's feet. "Oh, no," he gasped, when the gurney rolled past. "You don't think . . . ?"

"It's happening all over ag — "

The final syllable of Chace's sentence became one high-pitched scream as we watched the head beneath the sheet slowly turn and look at us.

About the Author

JAHNNA N. MALCOLM is really the pen name for the husband and wife team, Jahnna Beecham and Malcolm Hillgartner.

Both Jahnna and Malcolm believe they've had brushes with the supernatural. In fact, Jahnna lived in a haunted old farmhouse in Ohio when she was a child. When Jahnna and Malcolm are not writing scary books by the fireside, they enjoy appearing in plays.

Together they have written over thirty-five books for kids, including the Bad News Ballet series for Scholastic, and the mystery series Hart and Soul. Jahnna and Malcom currently live with their son Dash in an old log cabin on a lake in the northwestern corner of Montana . . . a perfect spot for ghostly appearances.